Redemption Lost

D1319155

WITHDRAWN

No longer the property of the
Boston Public Library.
Sale of this material benefits the Library.

Redemption Lost

Marc Avery

www.urbanbooks.net

Urban Books, LLC
300 Farmingdale Road, NY-Route 109
Farmingdale, NY 11735

Redemption Lost
Copyright © 2017 Marc Avery

All rights reserved. No part of this book may be reproduced in any form or by any means without prior consent of the Publisher, except brief quotes used in reviews.

ISBN 13: 978-1-62286-799-8
ISBN 10: 1-62286-799-8

First Mass Market Printing March 2017
Printed in the United States of America

10 9 8 7 6 5 4 3 2 1

This is a work of fiction. Any references or similarities to actual events, real people, living or dead, or to real locales are intended to give the novel a sense of reality. Any similarity in other names, characters, places, and incidents is entirely coincidental.

Distributed by Kensington Publishing Corp.
Submit Orders to:
Customer Service
400 Hahn Road
Westminster, MD 21157-4627
Phone: 1-800-733-3000
Fax: 1-800-659-2436

Redemption Lost

Marc Avery

Acknowledgments

There is a special group of women who were a huge part of this project:

Special thanks to: Shon Bacon, Locksie Locks, Carla Dean, Brenda Hampton, Ms. Toni Doe, Rakia Clark, English Ruler, Gloria Withers, Venay McKinney, Joyce Dickerson, Leila Jefferson, Shelia Goss, K. L. Brady, Rebecca from Hockessin Book Shelf, Marcela Landres, and Candace Cottrell.

Thank you all for your insight, critique, and expertise. This project wouldn't have come to fruition without you.

To my wife, Sharmina, thank you for sticking by me through everything, for being a constant positive influence, and listening to me ramble on about books.

I love you, Queen.

To my big brother/business partner/best friend, Keith, we've done enough talking; it's time to make moves. I'm swinging for the fences this time. I want my spot among the greats.

To my agent, Joylynn M. Ross, thank you for getting the deal done. They say timing is everything, and we couldn't have linked up at a better time. You're efficient and a woman of your word. I appreciate you and look forward to a prosperous relationship.

Last but not least, thank you, Carl Weber, for giving me a shot and the staff at Urban Books for helping me put this project together.

—MARC AVERY
www.iammarcavery.com

Dedication

This book is dedicated to my cousin,
Danielle "Pebbles" Thomas,
and my grandfather, Jimmy.

May you two rest in peace.

July

I heard my father and mother shouting at each other as I read *Screenwriting for Dummies*. I threw the book on my bed and rushed downstairs to see what the problem was.

These arguments were becoming a recurring theme lately. Every time my parents argued, my mother went through crazy mood swings. Normally, she gave out hugs and cheek kisses, but Senior had her acting cold and distant. They were so into their argument that they didn't even notice me standing there at the bottom of the stairs.

"Who is she?" my mother asked with her hands on her wide hips.

Senior smiled and shook his head. "Every day it's something new with you, Brenda. Don't you get tired of accusing me of shit? I know I'm sick of it."

"You come in the house at two in the morning smelling like perfume and liquor, and *you're* sick?" She looked at him like he had two heads. "You must have lost your damn mind."

Senior's forehead wrinkled in frustration. "I had a few Coronas at the bar. So what? I'm not guilty of anything."

"Explain this then." She handed him a letter.

Senior's eyes grew wide, and he sucked his teeth. "Why did you open my mail?" His voice cracked with emotion.

"What are you guys fighting for?" I asked, jumping into their conversation. This had gone far enough.

"Nothing, Junior. A small misunderstanding between your mother and me," Senior said, his hands flailing.

"Don't you lie to him, you son of a bitch," my mother said.

"Let me be clear," Senior began, pounding his fist into his palm to emphasize his point. "You wanted to find something, right? Unfortunately, you found what you were looking for. Don't blame me, Brenda." He walked off and went toward the steps.

"Can y'all calm down, please?" I asked, looking between them.

My mother's eyes narrowed to slits, and she followed after him. When Senior went to touch the banister, she grabbed his arm.

He yanked his arm free, and they stared each other down. Soon as Senior turned to go upstairs, my mother pushed him into the stairs.

After he stood up, he got in her face. Nothing could be heard but their heavy breathing.

"What you gonna do now, coward?" my mother asked and smirked.

Without warning, Senior slapped her in the mouth. She stumbled backward and landed on the floor.

In my seventeen years on earth, I had never seen Senior hit my mother. When I saw blood on her lip, I charged at him and knocked into his shoulder. At six foot three and 240 pounds, Senior, had me by two inches and thirty pounds, but I didn't give a shit. Once he put his hands on my mother, I had to do something.

"What the hell is your problem?" I asked him with my fists balled at my sides. We were nose to nose. I smelled hints of floral-scented perfume. Senior smelling like another woman's perfume made me sick to my stomach.

"Stay out of grown folks' business that doesn't concern you." He turned his back on me and walked away.

Something deep down inside of me snapped. I pushed him in the back, and he turned around and pushed me in the chest. Out of nowhere, he swung on me. I moved to my left and punched him in the jaw and the side of his head.

He touched his face in disbelief and gritted his teeth. Then, he punched me in the mouth and hit me in the stomach twice.

"You wanna act like an adult? I'll treat you like one."

Another punch to the stomach. He knocked the wind out of me, and I tasted blood on my lip.

"You must've lost your damn mind," Senior said, as I held my stomach in pain.

Once I caught my breath, I tackled him and knocked over the couch. I got on top of him and kept punching him in the face until my knuckles were bloody and my hands ached.

I stopped hitting him when my mother put her hand on my shoulder. "That's enough, Anthony." She held a kitchen knife in her other hand.

"You need to leave before I call the cops," she said to Senior in a fearful tone.

While lying on the ground and holding his jaw, Senior said, "I don't need this shit from either one of you. I'm out of here." He slowly got off the ground and went upstairs.

I circled the living room in a rage, mumbling to myself. I wanted to kick his ass some more.

"Try to calm down, baby," my mother said.

After a few minutes, Senior came downstairs with a small suitcase. I got in his face again.

"Wow, so you leaving us now?" I asked and shook my head in disappointment.

At that moment, I hated how much we looked alike. The long eyelashes, naturally curly hair, pointy nose, and light brown skin.

I even hated that we shared the same name, Anthony Edward Porter. I nicknamed him Senior, and he called me Junior. Both nicknames stuck with us over the years.

He shook his head and bit his lip. "You have a lot to learn about respect. I'm your father, and the shit you pulled today should make you ashamed of yourself. I'm not perfect, and neither are you. You remember that when it's your turn to be judged." I saw the hurt in his face as his eyes watered. Then he walked out the door. Something told me he was leaving for good.

I watched through the front window as he got into our piece-of-shit Toyota Camry with a donut on the wheel and peeled off up the street. His cologne and the other woman's perfume lingered in the living room long after he left.

All of his life lessons about family being number one were total bullshit. Obviously, my mother and I weren't that important because he left us without hesitation.

I went over to my mother who was slumped on the other couch with her chin to her chest.

"What did the letter say?" I put an arm around her and hugged her.

"Senior has another son," she whispered and let the tears fall.

I was stunned because now I had a baby brother out there in the world. Truthfully, I always wanted a sibling, but not under these circumstances. I was disappointed that Senior stepped out on my mother and had a mistress and another son. He abandoned us, and when he left our house, it was obvious that he chose his other family over us. How did my mother and I become so insignificant?

I wished like hell I could transfer the pain from my mother to me. Knowing Senior cheated was one thing. Seeing proof of his cheating ways pissed me off, and I'm sure my mother would never be the same. I wiped the tears from her cheek with my thumb.

I'm sure I would never be the same again, either.

Later that morning, a few hours after Senior left the house, I strolled through our tree-lined neighborhood. The sky was pink and orange, and the clouds looked like cotton balls bunched together. The air outside was cool and crisp despite it being July. It was peaceful out there, and taking a walk allowed me to clear my head.

Thinking about Senior, I had so many questions. Why did he cheat on my mother? Did he love us anymore? What would I do the next time I saw him? Would there be a next time? Would we speak again? What would my life become without him?

I circled back around the block and lumbered home. Back inside the house, I stood by my parents' half-opened bedroom door, eavesdropping on my mother's phone conversation.

She blamed herself and said she should've been more attentive to Senior's needs. I wanted to rush inside their room and shake her for blaming herself for his bullshit. I grew tired of her making excuses for him. Instead, I let her vent to whoever she was on the phone with and went into my bedroom.

I vowed to make it big in Hollywood so my mother would never again have to depend on a man for shit. She was my responsibility now. On my watch, she would never have to struggle again.

Back in high school, I had to write a screenplay for a class project and found out I enjoyed writing way more than I expected to. By the time I graduated from high school in June, I had finished two crime fiction screenplays, one named *Compromised* and the other named *Cold-Blooded*.

At first, I wanted to make some money for myself when I eventually sold the screenplays to somebody. Now with Senior gone, I wanted to make money for me and my mother.

Between Senior abandoning us and my mother blaming herself for his actions, I needed a drink. I grabbed a bottle of vodka out of my nightstand and took it to the head.

My love for vodka started in the eleventh grade. At an unsupervised house party, I got caught in a dare to take shots of liquor. Soon after, I became addicted to drinking.

I hoped the vodka would dull the pain of Senior choosing to be with another family over us.

September

On a breezy Friday afternoon in September, I came back to Philly from New York City. I had enjoyed an all-expense-paid screenwriting retreat courtesy of Señor. It was a gift for having a 4.0 grade point average and being the valedictorian of my graduating class. The pricey two-week trip represented the last meaningful deed the man did for me.

The retreat's workshops educated me on tightening scenes, eliminating fluff, and finding a unique voice of my own. I soaked up every word and committed every tip to memory. Then, I ate until I had to loosen my belt at the nightly buffet.

After we ate dinner, they allowed us to explore Times Square. The giant billboards. The bright lights. The fleet of Yellow Cabs. The smell of roasted peanuts, gyros, and grilled hot dogs. The people who roamed the streets. All of those things inspired me to write. Sometimes I didn't sleep a full eight hours because the ideas wouldn't stop coming to me. Having real-life things to draw from helped me to write things easier. The retreat also gave me the perfect distraction from thinking about Senior's abuse and him abandoning us.

I got off the cigarette-smelling Greyhound bus feeling stiff. My legs were cramped for most of the ninety-minute bus ride. At least I got to talk to a retired homicide detective. He gave me a lot of insight on police procedure that I used in my screenplay.

After I used the bathroom in the bus station, I walked around the corner and took the regular bus home.

When I walked in the house, I heard my mother talking loudly on the phone upstairs. Then, I noticed a pile of envelopes on the dining-room table. Most of the envelopes said *Final Notice* in bold red. I looked at the envelopes quizzically because I assumed the bills were being paid.

I hit play to listen to the messages on the answering machine. All five of the voice mails said, "This is an attempt to collect a debt." I pushed stop on the answering machine and went into the kitchen. Dishes filled the sink, and the trash overflowed in the trash can. Down in the basement, I found clothes all over the floor in the laundry room. Obviously, something was going on.

I went all the way up to my mother's bedroom and stood by the door to eavesdrop on her conversation.

"I don't know how long I can keep this a secret. Girl, what the hell am I going to do with another child?"

My eyebrows shot up in surprise. I rushed into her bedroom, and shock crossed her face.

"Leslie, let me call you right back." She fumbled with her cell phone before ending the call and looking at me. "Anthony, baby, when did you get here?"

Ignoring her question, I asked, "How far along are you?"

She became silent.

I came over and patted her on the shoulder supportively. "I'm here for you."

She looked up at me, and her eyes watered. "I'm two and a half months."

"Why didn't you tell me?" I asked softly.

"I didn't want to burden you with my problems. Our situation is stressful enough."

"Your stress is my stress too. I'm a big boy. I can take a lot. Is there anything else you want to tell me?"

She nodded. "We're behind a couple thousand with the bills . . . and a couple months with the mortgage." She avoided eye contact with me.

I sat next to her on the bed. "Before I left for the retreat, you said we would be okay even though Senior left. Is that still true?" I asked, trying not to think pessimistically.

"Of course, baby. I'm going to figure a way out of this for us. We won't be down forever." She grabbed my hand and looked me in the eyes. "I promise."

So far, my mother hadn't ever lied to me, so I took her words to heart.

I switched subjects. "What happened with the dishes and the laundry room?"

"The truth?"

"Of course."

"Sometimes your mother can be lazy."

I pulled her into a hug. "I still love you, though."

"I love you too, baby."

In the middle of our tender moment, the electricity cut off.

"I'll get some candles from downstairs," I said before I traveled through the darkened hallway.

My mother's words echoed in my head as I went down the steps. *"I'm going to figure a way out of this for us."*

I sure hoped so because we were in a bad spot.

October

Since we didn't have any electricity, I went to the Free Library with my flash drive and used their computer to edit my screenplays and search for jobs. Because I felt the pressure to step up in Senior's absence, I stayed at the library from open to close five days out of the week. The majority of the time, I got the, "I regret to inform you . . ." e-mails from employers.

Between our living situation and the nonexistent job opportunities, I was hitting the liquor bottle hard. I'd drink after breakfast, lunch, and dinner. Sometimes, I got lit when I went on the job interviews. My nerves were shot, and vodka calmed me down.

When I left the library that night, all I wanted to do was have a drink and go to sleep.

As I rounded the corner, I saw a group of people in front of my house. I immediately thought something happened to my mother. I broke into a sprint. My heart shattered into a million pieces when I saw it—our belongings on the sidewalk displayed for everyone to see.

Whoever put our stuff outside didn't bother putting it in boxes. Everything lay haphazardly on the sidewalk with our dressers and end tables. With watery eyes and a heavy heart, I pushed through the crowd and ran up the stairs to find a padlock and an eviction notice on our front door.

Feeling naked and vulnerable, I came back down the steps. "All of you need to mind your own fucking business!" I yelled at them before they all dispersed.

I had never felt more alone in my life. I called my mom's cell after I noticed the missed calls from her. My cell phone had been on vibrate at the library.

"I'm so sorry you found out like this," she said somberly.

My shoulders slumped as I sat on our steps. "What are we going to do now?" I blew out a frustrated breath.

"For now, we're going to stay with Aunt Leslie."

"That's nice of her to let us stay there."

"Yeah. She's a lifesaver."

"Yes, she is," I said, smiling weakly.

"You still remember how to get here?"

"Yeah. I'll be there as soon as I can."

After I ended the call, I went and searched through our stuff and found a loose trash bag. I stuffed the bag with family pictures. When I looked at a picture of me, my mother, and Senior in Ocean City, I thought of happier times. All of our family vacations. All of the times we went to the movies. All of our family game nights. Now, all of it was gone, and nothing would ever be the same.

The more I thought about our belongings, the more I didn't want any of this stuff anymore. It represented the past, and I wanted to focus on the future.

I spared our home one last glance before I walked to the bus stop.

I took a bus and a train to get to Aunt Leslie's apartment in North Philly. Abandoned buildings were scattered on her block. As I walked past the Chinese restaurant, there was a group of guys smoking. Weed smoke and fried shrimp lit up my nostrils.

Her two-bedroom apartment was on the third floor, and the hallway smelled like French fries and bleach.

Aunt Leslie answered the door smiling. She was a thick woman, and when she hugged me, she almost crushed me.

"It's good to see you, but I wish it was under different circumstances," she said.

"Me too, Auntie."

"I'll leave you two alone," Aunt Leslie said and stepped away so my mother and I could talk.

I put the trash bag down by the closet and sat on the couch next to my mother. "How long can we stay here?" I asked.

"Leslie didn't give me a timetable. We can stay here until we get back on our feet."

"I hope we're not here too long."

"Me either, baby."

"What are we going to do for money?"

My mother sighed. "Leslie is going to cover us as much as she can, and I'm waiting to hear back from a couple of jobs I applied to."

"I'm playing the waiting game too with these jobs."

"I'm prayerful that we will get the job calls sooner than later." She touched my shoulder and smiled weakly.

I looked into her eyes. "I'm going to do whatever it takes to get a job. With Senior gone, I'm the man of the house, and I'm going to take care of you."

"Baby, you don't have to worry about me. You get a job and take care of yourself. Mama will be okay, and so will you. You hear me?"

"I hear you."

I stood. "I'm going out for a walk to clear my head. I shouldn't be gone long," I said and headed for the door.

"Okay. If you go to the store, can you bring me back an iced honey bun?" she asked.

"Sure thing."

When I got outside of the building, my cell phone rang. An unknown number popped up on my caller ID.

"Who this?" I asked.

"Hello, I'm Jessica from Phaedra's Soul Food. I'm calling to see if you're still interested in the position."

"Yes, ma'am, I am."

"Can you come in for an interview tomorrow morning?"

I smiled like the Grinch. "Absolutely."

Initially, I planned to drown my sorrows with vodka. Now the drink would be celebratory.

October

I sat in the waiting area of Phaedra's Soul Food restaurant waiting for the manager to show up. The vodka I drank earlier had me sweating like a whore in church. I looked at the walls and the ground and blew out nervous breaths. A soft voice called for me and broke me out of my trance.

"Mr. Porter." The voice belonged to a thick, milk chocolate-skinned woman with the body of a porn star.

"Hello, ma'am," I said politely. I tried my hardest not to stare at her cantaloupe-sized breasts.

"You don't have to be formal with me, Anthony. Call me Phaedra."

"Okay. I can do that." I held the door open for her to pass through first.

Her tropical-scented perfume made me horny. She looked sexy in her revealing top and tight jeans that showed off her giant ass.

Inside her office, silver-framed pictures of her and other people who were mostly in suits covered her walls. Seeing how junky her office was, I knew she probably put a lot of hours in at the restaurant.

"I read over your application and nothing jumped out at me right away . . ." She paused.

Remaining professional, I looked her in the eye and listened closely.

"However, the ideal candidate paragraph you wrote showed me your passion. You're excellent with words, sir." She smiled and showed two perfect rows of teeth.

I goofily smiled back at her. "Thank you very much."

"The job is yours if you want it."

"When do I start?" I asked eagerly.

"Next Tuesday."

After I left my job interview, I went back to Aunt Leslie's feeling like I hit the lottery jackpot. As soon as I got into the apartment, I broke into a silly dance. Being able to make my own money made me feel like a man. This was the first step toward helping my mother get back on her feet. If I did some OT, maybe I could save up enough money, and we could find a cheap apartment of our own.

My mother came out of the kitchen and smiled when she saw me clapping and spinning around.

"Boy, what are you doing?" she asked and walked over to me.

"I got a job today."

My mother's eyes grew wide with excitement, and she high-fived me. "Congratulations, baby."

"Thank you, Mom."

We sat on the couch.

"Where are you going to be working at?"

"Phaedra's Soul Food."

"Now, I know I can get me a discount, right?" she asked and laughed.

"Of course," I said, grinning.

"Look, baby, I'm going to go and take a nap. If you get hungry, there's chicken fingers in the freezer."

"Okay."

She made a beeline for the bedroom.

I got on Aunt Leslie's laptop and edited one of my screenplays. When it got dark outside, I stopped typing and decided to go to the basketball courts.

Once I got on the avenue, I bought a bag of cheese curls and a Red Bull from the corner store.

The block was lively. Two shapely women argued while a man stood in between them grinning. Farther down the street, a skinny black man with a raggedy beard was hawking bootleg cologne and perfumes. As I went to cross the street, a guy on a dirt bike zoomed by me popping a wheelie.

A few blocks later, I finished my cheese curls and Red Bull and stepped on the blacktop like I belonged there. I stood near the gate with a few other spectators.

A white guy complained to another player about picking a final teammate to play with.

Seeing my opportunity, I walked up on the group of players unannounced and said, "I'll play."

"Did I ask you to play?" the white guy asked and got in my face.

I looked him in the eye and smirked. "You scared or something, chump?" I taunted him, and the people on the court showered him with *oohs!*

Unexpectedly, he hit me in the stomach with the ball, knocking the wind out of me.

"Watch your mouth when you come on my court, bro," he said with cold eyes and a harsh tone.

I caught my breath after a few moments. "Stop being a bitch and check the rock up."

Soon as we got into the flow of the game, I knew they played dirty. That was right up my alley. I pretended everybody on the other team was Senior. I made sure to be ultra-aggressive. When I got the chance, I swung my elbows at their faces and tripped them when they came in the paint.

The white guy who threw the ball at me hugged me on defense. I hit him with my shoulder and elbowed him in the jaw. As his head whipped back, I drove the lane and made the game-winning shot on a layup off the backboard. Claps and cheers rained down on me. I felt like King Kong.

I smirked, flung the basketball at the gate, and strolled toward the exit. Someone approached me from behind. On the defensive, I turned around and pushed him in the chest. I was ready to fight somebody.

The white guy put his hands up defensively. "I come in peace, bro." He stuck out his hand.

"I'm sorry, man." We shook hands. "I'm Anthony, by the way."

"I'm Paul. And I didn't mean any disrespect by what I said earlier. I got caught up in the competition out there."

"Trust me, I understand."

"I can't remember the last time I lost to anybody. You got some skills, bro. You most definitely held your own out there."

"Maybe we can do the best two out of three next time," I said and smiled.

"Definitely, bro." Paul threw the basketball to one of the players on the court. "Take my number so we can link up."

I punched his number into my cell phone.

"Good meeting you, man," I said.

"Same here, bro."

We shook hands again and went our separate ways.

Maybe living with Aunt Leslie wouldn't be so bad after all.

December

Working at Phaedra's was dope because my coworkers helped me through my adjustment period, and they were good people. My official job title was floater because I floated between tasks. So far, I had greeted and seated customers, prepped the food, shopped for food, taste tested the food, cleaned the bathroom, swept the main floor, washed the dishes, and I helped Phaedra lock up at night sometimes.

After work, I came off the El train around 6:00 p.m. and walked to Aunt Leslie's apartment. To fight off the bitter cold outside, I zipped my winter jacket up to the top and pulled my hat over my ears.

Once I grabbed the mail out of the mailbox, I went inside and put the envelopes on the dining-room table. I took my hat and coat off and sat at the computer.

Since I finally finished with my screenplay edits, I created a cookie-cutter Web site that would showcase my work. For two hours, I researched agents' e-mail addresses, Web sites, phone numbers, and pitch-session opportunities.

There wasn't a pitch-session opportunity in my area until next year, so I stuck to sending out specs to people in the film business that looked legit and had a working e-mail address.

After I finished my research, I lay on the couch and eventually fell asleep. Unfortunately, my mother woke me up when she came in the house.

I sat up and rubbed my eyes. "Is everything okay?" I asked.

"Yes, it is," my mother said and smiled.

"What's up then?"

"Senior sent us a check for $3,000." She smiled so hard I thought her teeth would crack.

The mention of his name made my chest swell up with anger.

We hadn't heard from him since he abandoned us. I called and left him so many voice mails, I lost count. After a while, he disconnected his phone number. I even went to his job, and his manager told me he quit. No matter what, my mother and I deserved some closure.

"We don't need that coward's money," I yelled and jumped off the couch.

"You need to calm down," my mother yelled back.

"I'm sorry if I don't share your same level of enthusiasm," I said sarcastically.

"Contrary to popular belief, we *do* need his money if we eventually want to move out of here."

"I'll work OT and save up for us to move. We don't need anything from him."

"And your minimum-wage job is going to help us do that?" she asked in an icy tone.

"At least I *have* a job." I matched her pettiness.

She shook her head. "You must've fell and bumped your head."

"I didn't bump anything. We been here a few months, and I don't see much job progress on *your* part."

She stepped closer to me. "I won't have you disrespecting me."

"I'm not disrespecting you. I'm telling you the truth. I'm not a slacker like you are."

"You're treading on thin ice, boy."

"Whatever. I think you need to focus on getting a job instead of being hyped about a handout."

"Senior is at least trying to right his wrongs, and we're getting the money we deserve."

"Fuck him and fuck his money. I can't be bought, but I see you can."

She slapped me so hard my lip split and started bleeding.

I touched the blood on my lip and looked at her in disbelief.

"I've dealt with the BS from Senior, and I won't deal with it from you too."

I gave her a death stare before I stormed out of the house. Our disagreement let me know just how messed up things were. All I wanted was to feel a sense of normalcy again.

I guess deep down, I just wanted Senior to come back instead of him writing us checks.

March

'Three months later, my mother and I found a new spot back in West Philly. Wasn't as nice as our old house, but it was comfortable, affordable, and I had more space in my bedroom.

I would always be thankful to Aunt Leslie for helping us get back on our feet. Out of the kindness of her heart, she made her home our home. I was sad when we left.

In the last three months, Senior sent us over $9,000 in checks. Although I didn't want his help, he did enable us to move into our own space. I wasn't thrilled about it, but I learned to appreciate the man's gesture.

When he sent us letters, he never put his return address on them, and all the letter would say is *"I'll send more next month."* A part of me wanted Senior to man up and call us or at least tell us where he lived.

It burned my soul that, by virtue of his monthly checks, he still controlled our household. I wasn't making enough money yet, and it pissed me off that I couldn't take care of us.

My mother seemed to be happy, and I didn't want to rain on her parade, but I would feel much better when she got her own job.

I turned eighteen in our new house, and I hadn't made any plans other than opening up a checking and savings account.

I went into the kitchen and was surprised to find eggs, potatoes, and bacon waiting for me in the microwave. When I went back to the dining room, I found a blue envelope lying on the dining-room table. I rubbed my hands together in anticipation.

When I opened the birthday card, $200 fell out. The message inside the card read:

Try not to spend it all in one place
Love, Mommy

I thought it would be cool to have a girlfriend to spend this money with. Hadn't really had time for a relationship or the desire since my mother and Senior were in the middle of their drama. Who wants to bring someone special into that mess? Besides . . . I'm not really experienced with girls per se.

No sooner than the thought left my mind, my boy Paul called and said he was on the way over. I complained that I wanted to chill, but he was having none of it. Within twenty minutes, I was dressed, on the street, and ready to hang out with him.

After some more basketball games and a few trips to Dave & Buster's, Paul and I became real tight. What made us connect even more were our personal losses. Neither of our fathers were in our lives. Paul's loss went deeper than mine. His father, a war veteran, had a severe case of PTSD and was prescribed medicine to help him cope. Unfortunately, he went off of his meds and ended up killing his wife and himself.

We weren't just friends. I considered him family.

Plus, he was older than me, so I enjoyed the stories he told me about his life experiences, especially with girls. He told the best stories.

I looked up to him. At twenty-two years old, he owned his own vehicle, had a dope apartment in University City, and worked as a personal trainer.

I aspired to have my shit together like he did.

Before I left the house, I checked the Yahoo! e-mail app on my phone to see if any agents had e-mailed me. Unfortunately, I had a bunch of e-mails that said, "This isn't right for us at this time."

Those e-mails had been the norm for the last couple of months. Despite the rejection, I vowed to keep on pushing. I shook the negativity off and focused on having a good time on my birthday.

When I got outside, I hopped in the passenger seat of his gray Ford Explorer, and we shook hands.

"Let me tell you how this girl tried to play me last night." He went right in.

"What happened now?" I asked, excited to hear his story about a woman.

"She said she don't sleep around on the first night. I told her I don't pay for food or the movies on the first night, either. Needless to say, she let me hit by the end of the night," he smirked.

I shook my head. "So, being a dick really works with women, huh?" I was stunned because I thought being a gentleman got you the girls.

"Pretty much." He shrugged like it was nothing. "Speaking of women, when's the last time you went on a date?"

Embarrassment hit me like a sucker punch in the jaw, and I looked out the window. "I've never been on a date before." My stomach bubbled with nervousness because I knew he would think I was a sucker.

"*What?* Next thing you're going to tell me is you're a virgin too." He laughed. He stopped laughing when I didn't say anything back to him.

"Hold up a minute." His eyes got big. "You have desert dick? Say it isn't so."

"Ha-ha-ha. Very funny . . . I need to stop at the bank, and then we need to get something to eat."

Paul wouldn't stop laughing at me. "Say no more, bro."

Paul parked along South Street after we left the bank. Then we got in the line at Ishkabibble's and ordered cheesesteaks when it was our turn.

We ate inside the truck.

"Slow down, Anthony, before you choke on your food," Paul said as he took a bite of his steak.

"Shut up, man. I'm hungry as hell," I mumbled with a mouth full of food.

A thick and attractive woman walking across the street caught my eye. She had honey-roasted skin, curves for days, and large breasts that could barely be contained by her business suit top.

Paul caught me staring at her with a goofy smile on my face. "She's cute. Bet you twenty dollars you don't have the heart to speak to her, bro," he taunted me.

My heart beat double time as the anxiety kicked in. Faking confidence, I took him up on the bet. I couldn't look like a chump in front of him, no matter how shook I felt on the inside.

"I'll take your twenty dollars," I said cockily.

I hopped out of the truck and ran after her.

By the time I caught up with her, I had to catch my breath.

"So, what's your name, miss?" I approached her from behind, and butterflies fluttered around my stomach.

She turned around and said, "None of your damn bus—"

When we made eye contact, she softened her approach.

"I'm sorry. I didn't mean to be rude."

I smiled. "No need to apologize. I know guys can be a little overaggressive."

"Boy, you have no idea." She smiled warmly. "My name is Essence."

"Nice to meet you, Essence. I'm Anthony."

I extended my hand to her, and in one fell swoop, the rest of my life changed.

"You're a very beautiful woman, and I had to come over here," I complimented her. I couldn't ignore her curvy hips, thick thighs, and long hair.

"Thank you. You aren't too bad your damn self," she said and openly licked her lips.

Her passion fruit perfume turned me on.

"Walk with me for a minute."

"Okay."

I grabbed her hand and walked off of South Street.

"So, Anthony, tell me something about yourself."

"I was the valedictorian in high school, and I'm also a screenwriter."

"Okay. I see you, boy."

"How about you? Tell me something about yourself." I tossed the question back her way.

"I don't like to brag, but I'm a regional manager for TD Bank, and I have a bachelor's degree in finance."

"All right, big time."

She had brains and beauty. I'm glad Paul suggested we hang out or I would've never met her. Everything happened for a reason.

"Look, Essence, I'm going to be up front with you. You're a beautiful woman, and I'd like to get to know you better." I laid all my cards out on the table.

We stopped walking.

"Is that right?" she asked with a raised eyebrow and a hand on her hip.

"Yup." Anxiety hit me hard again, and my heart almost beat out of my chest.

"How old are you, Anthony?" She squinted her eyes at me.

I blew out a nervous breath and prepared for the backlash. "Eighteen."

"Boy, are you trying to get me arrested?" She smiled and shook her head.

I couldn't help but smile too. "No. Not at all. How old are you?"

"I'm twenty-seven."

"That's not a problem. I like older women anyway." I shrugged because our age difference meant nothing to me.

"You're lucky you cute or else I would've bounced on you," she said seriously.

I involuntarily licked my lips. "So, can you take my number?" I asked eagerly.

"Slow down there, cowboy." She grabbed my cell phone from me. "You can take mine." She programmed her number into my phone and walked back to her truck. "We'll talk again soon."

I rushed back to Paul's truck smiling from ear to ear.

"Can I have my twenty dollars, please?" I asked with my hand out.

Paul passed me the twenty-dollar bill and said, "She was bad. I'm proud of you, bro."

"Thanks, man. If you didn't challenge me, I might not have gotten out of the truck."

"That's what friends are for," he said, and we bumped fists.

Should I call her tonight? I thought on the ride home. *Naaaah. She'll think I'm desperate. But if I don't call . . . maybe she'll think I'm not interested. But I've got to play it cool . . . or Paul won't let me hear the end of it. But then again, I don't have much experience, so I don't want to rush. I don't know what to do.*

Sleep.

I decided I would sleep on the decision.

April

To avoid seeming too thirsty, I waited three weeks to call Essence. Around eight o'clock one night, I dialed her number and hung up before I could punch in the last digit. Finally, I took a deep breath and made the call. Her sexy voice floated through the receiver.

All she said was hello, and my heart was beating through my chest . . . and something else was trying to get out of my pants.

"Uh . . . hello. Can I speak to Essence, please?" I circled the living room, feeling nervous all of a sudden.

"This is she."

"It's Anthony. We met on South Street last month."

"Did we now?"

"Yes. I don't forget attractive women very often."

"So I'm your type, then?"

I sat on the couch and tried to relax. "Yes, as a matter of fact, you're definitely my type."

"We have something in common, then."

She didn't hang up on me, so I knew I was in.

"So, what do you like to do for fun?" I asked.

"I like to hit the mall or catch a good movie. I'm a simple girl, really. What do you like to get into?"

"I mostly like to read, write, and watch sports. Regular guy stuff. Nothing major."

"Most guys I know only read the back of the cereal box."

I couldn't help but smile. "Where are you from?"

"I'm from West Baltimore, and I assume you're from Philly."

"Born and raised," I said proudly.

Losing total track of time, we talked until the low battery signal sounded on my cell phone. It was close to 10:00 p.m. by now. She had me sprung after one conversation.

Crossing my fingers, I asked, "Can I take you out to dinner sometime?"

"How about Friday around seven?" she offered.

"Sounds good to me. Looking forward to it."

"All right. We'll talk again soon."

When I got off the phone with Essence, I heard my mother yell my name.

I rushed upstairs and into her bedroom. She sat on the edge of the bed with her hands on her knees rocking back and forth.

"Grab my bag out of the closet. This baby is coming tonight," she said in obvious pain.

"Do you want me to call Aunt Leslie?" I was concerned for her and excited at the same time. I always wanted a brother, and now he was on his way.

"No, baby. I called her already. She'll be here soon to come and get us."

We stormed inside the ER entrance of the hospital. The hospital's staff helped my mother into a wheelchair. With urgent footsteps, they pushed her through the brightly lit halls to the maternity ward with Aunt Leslie following closely behind them. Aunt Leslie barked orders to the orderlies as they tried to do their jobs.

Personally, I couldn't stomach childbirth since I had already been scarred for life from those videos they forced us to watch in health class, so I went to the lounge area. Already knowing I was limited in my choices, I skimmed through outdated magazines and looked at TV. Changing the channel wasn't an option. I had to watch a made-for-television movie.

After sitting there for a while and playing games on my cell phone, I dozed off. My aunt's text message woke me up hours later, and I suddenly became alert.

He's here! Come on up here and see him! We are in room 5C!

With my curiosity at an all-time high, I hopped out of my seat, burst through the double doors of the lounge area, and sprinted to the elevator. Once inside the elevator, I frantically pressed the button for the fifth floor like I would get there faster. The ride felt like forever until the doors finally opened, and I bolted out of the elevator.

Careful not to make any noise, I tiptoed into the cold hospital room and became choked up at the sight of my little brother. Aunt Leslie handed him to me. I instantly felt protective of him.

"What's his name?" I asked as I cradled him.

"His name is Michael." She smiled and put her hair into a ponytail. "Sleepyhead over there did a great job, didn't she?" She pointed to my mother.

I nodded and smiled. "Yes, she did."

I cried tears of joy. My heart swelled with pride when I looked at my little brother and mother. It was my job to protect them.

With Senior gone, I had become the man of the house. They needed me, and I vowed to be there for them in any way I could.

I was all they had in this world, and they were all I had too.

April

Three days later, my mother brought Michael home after the hospital had discharged her. I circled the living room. Essence and I were going out to eat, and I had a bunch of nervous energy rolling around inside of me.

I was also torn because I knew my mother was dead tired and needed a break from the baby. I hopped off the couch as the front door opened, and she walked in. With my arms outstretched, I snatched Michael and his baby bag away from her.

"Hello to you too." She shook her head and smiled.

"Sorry, Mom." I kissed her on the cheek.

While I talked gibberish to Michael, he gave me the twitching smile all babies give when they're that young. I put the bag down by the couch.

I cradled him as I walked in the kitchen with my mother. She got a bottle of water out of the refrigerator.

"I might stay over at Paul's house tonight. I'll call or text you to let you know if I do."

"Hold on a minute. You need to stay here to watch your brother so I can get some damn rest," she frowned.

"Michael's my brother, not my son, Mom. I'm a teenager, growing into a man, and I need to get me some sooner or later. I'm hoping sooner."

"Everything is about Anthony twenty-four-seven," she said with her arms flailing. "You can be so damn selfish sometimes. Just like your father."

"Wow. That's where you decide to go?" My eyes narrowed to slits. "Fine. I'll stay here until he falls asleep. Then I'm out."

She shook her head. "You just don't get it, do you?"

I scrunched up my face. "What exactly don't I get?"

"I need you to be here in case he wakes up in the middle of the night." She gave me a look like I should've known better.

I blew out a frustrated breath. "Fine. I'll stay here with him."

"It's okay. Don't worry about it," she said and took the baby from me. He started crying.

"Wait a min—"

She cut me off. "I said it was okay." Then she stormed past me and went upstairs.

I was ready to reschedule my date with Essence and stay home with Michael. However, my mother decided to be difficult.

Frustrated, I texted Paul, and he agreed to come and pick me up.

Thirty minutes later, he came around the corner blasting the song, "Beverly Hills" by Weezer. I hopped inside his truck, and we shook hands.

"You all ready for your big date with Essence?" he asked with a big grin.

"My mom just pissed me off. She wanted me to stay home and watch Michael." I rubbed my forehead.

"Bro, get off that. Focus on getting some from Essence. Tonight's your night. I can feel it."

"I hear you, but I can't believe she called me selfish. Like I haven't been there when she needed me?"

"Let it go, Anthony." He patted me on the shoulder. "Let it go."

I tried my best to block my mother's bullshit out of my mind. "You got any pointers for me?"

He nodded and smiled. "That's more like it. Make sure you pull her chair out. Wherever you go, make sure you can afford their prices. Stick to the basics. Less is more." He paused. "And do not let her pay the check or the tip because she'll offer to do so. It's a test that you better not fail."

"Okay. I think I got this." I nodded with blind confidence. On the outside, I played it cool. Inside, I began to panic. I didn't want to look like a fool in front of her.

Paul pulled up to Essence's row home in West Philadelphia, and then let the truck run.

"You've got one shot to make a good first impression on this girl. Do your boy proud."

We fist-bumped with each other before he peeled off down the street. After taking a deep breath, I pressed her doorbell and stepped back. When she walked out of the house, my jaw dropped to the ground. Her brown hair framed her face, and her dress lay on her skin perfectly. Even in the dim light outside, her matching manicure and pedicure stood out. She impressed the hell out of me with her whole getup.

Her perfume became trapped inside of my clothes when we hugged. We walked to her truck. She hit the button on her key fob and unlocked the doors.

I rushed to open the driver-side door before I jumped in the passenger side of her truck.

"Thank you. You're quite the gentleman."

"You're very welcome."

Making sure to take Paul's advice, I kept the restaurant real simple. We ended up at Applebee's in Center City. I made sure I held the restaurant door open for Essence.

Before we were seated, I hurried to the bathroom and guzzled the miniature bottle of vodka I had with me. Once the warmness from the liquor spread throughout my body, I got myself straight in the mirror and walked back out to the main floor.

Back at the table, I stuffed the handkerchief into the collar of my shirt and kept moving my silverware around on the table.

Seeing this, Essence laughed at me.

"What's so funny?" I asked defensively.

"You can put your napkin in your lap, boy. You don't put it in your shirt." She covered her mouth as she continued to laugh at me.

I shook my head and hoped I didn't blow my opportunity with her. I was a ball of nervous energy.

Half an hour later, we finished what I felt like was a pretty crappy dinner. I knocked over the pitcher of water and almost choked on my food when I laughed while eating.

"I'm glad we got to chill together," I said.

"Me too. Despite what happened earlier, we got the night back on track," she said, acknowledging my clumsiness.

I couldn't stop thinking about how thick her thighs were in her short dress. I thought Essence was bad when we first met, but under the bright lights in the restaurant, she was even badder. Long hair and big breasts did it for me, and she had both.

After we finished our conversation, I left a tip for our server, and we left the restaurant holding hands.

We pulled up to Paul's apartment building, and she kept the engine running.

Feeling hot all of a sudden, I stared at the crack of her breasts and licked my lips. I wanted to squeeze her breasts so damn bad. "I hope we can go out to eat, again." I swallowed hard.

"Oh, we definitely are. You were a good boy tonight." She reminded me of a naughty school-teacher when she said that.

With lust in the air, I closed my eyes and went in for a kiss. I missed her lips and kissed her chin. She grabbed my face to make sure our lips connected the next time.

My first kiss.

"I'll call you tomorrow," she said.

"Okay," I said, feeling superhorny. She caressed my cheek before I got out of the truck. I almost floated into Paul's apartment building I felt so good. My mother sent me a text message and immediately pissed me off . . . again.

Thanks for nothing, son.

I didn't respond to her text message and put my phone back in my pocket.

Man, I wished I could've gone back to Essence's place and had sex with her. It would've been the perfect cherry on top of my night. When she kissed me, I wanted to go further. Now, all I could do was imagine what sex would be like with her.

My phone buzzed again, and I hoped it wasn't my mother bothering me with some more of her nonsense.

Essence sent me a text message.

When I saw the topless selfie she sent me, I needed a cold shower.

May

I went from my job to Essence's house, picking up a bag of groceries on the way . . . all her favorites that she asked for and a few extras.

She took the grocery bags from me and went into the kitchen. I loved how her place was laid out with black leather furniture and smelled like clean linen air freshener. Her flat-screen TV hung on the wall, and everything had its own place.

She leaned against the breakfast nook in the kitchen, and I grabbed her by the waist. I kissed her exposed shoulder blade before she pulled away from me and laughed uncomfortably. Her awkward vibe threw me off.

This was the norm the last couple of weeks. I had been hinting around about sex, and she was having none of it. We would kiss, and then when I touched her or went for the French kiss, she rejected me.

At first, I thought I was tripping too hard, but not having sex became a problem for me. I really liked her, and I thought you had sex with people you liked. Maybe I was wrong about her liking me as much as I liked her. She was playing mind games, and I wasn't the one.

I thought if I did nice things for her, like buying groceries or cooking for her, she would eventually give in, but I was dead wrong.

"So what's on the menu?" Essence asked, purposely avoiding my touch.

"I'll surprise you with something," I said, smiling, even though I was pissed off.

I made us six-cheese spinach and grilled chicken pasta. I got the recipe from Google.

"This food is good, boy. We have to add chef to your résumé," she complimented me on the meal with a mouth full of food.

I picked at my food because I had lost my appetite. "Thank you," I said dryly.

"What's the matter with you?" Essence asked. In my opinion, she knew full well what was wrong with me.

"You know what's wrong with me. Don't play dumb."

Essence put her fork down. "Listen, Anthony, you're cute and everything, but what am I supposed to do with your young ass?" She giggled.

I couldn't see the humor in what she said. "Be real with me. Am I doing something wrong? If so, I'll stop."

"I like hanging out with you. I really do. To be honest, I don't want to rush into anything, and then regret the decision later."

Her words hit me like an uppercut.

"We don't have to be in love or anything," I offered.

"Sex is very complicated," she countered.

"So, you're telling me you don't want me?" I touched her hand, and she pulled away from me.

"Maybe I should leave then." I gritted my teeth.

"Maybe you should."

My nerves wouldn't settle down, and my mind was spinning a million miles a minute. We basically did what couples do. We fooled around. We even went out on a few more dates, talked on the phone for hours, and spent a lot of time together. I thought I did everything I needed to do to win her over.

With a bitter taste in my mouth, I grabbed my jacket off the chair and stormed out of her house.

After I left Essence's house, I went back home and tried to avoid speaking with my mother. I saw her at the dining-room table with an open pizza box, and I tried to rush upstairs. Noticing this, she gave me the side eye and told me to come and sit down with her. We rarely ate dinner together, so I knew something was up. By the look on her face, whatever she had to say was pretty serious this time.

"You've been acting strange the last couple of weeks. Are you seeing someone?"

I sat down at the table and grabbed a slice of pepperoni pizza. "Why do you assume I'm seeing someone?"

"You've been spending a lot of time on the phone lately, you're wearing cologne now, and you smell like perfume."

I sighed. "Well, Detective Porter, her name is Essence, and she's twenty-seven. Happy now?" I bit into my slice of pizza.

"I'm not sure I heard you right. This girl you're seeing is twenty-seven years old?"

I nodded.

"How come she can't find someone her own age?"

"We aren't in a relationship, if you must know. It's not that serious."

"I've heard it all before. Older women eat young boys like you up for breakfast."

"That might apply to other people, but not me," I said matter-of-factly.

"You're so hardheaded sometimes. I'm trying to save you from heartache, baby. Just trust me on this one."

"Just because Senior was older than you?" I said guessing where she was headed.

"Exactly. I know about this type of situation firsthand."

"Our situations are nothing alike. I got this."

She shook her head and smirked. "I see your little girlfriend got you smelling yourself right now."

"Whatever. I told you it's not that serious," I said and stormed up to my room and slammed the door shut.

Out of nowhere, I heard Michael crying. I had been getting up in the middle of the night to tend to him for the last few months. I knew my mother heard him crying, but I would take care of him anyway.

Shaking my head, I went into my mother's bedroom and picked Michael up out of his bassinet. He cried for a few more moments before I gave him his pacifier and patted him on the back. Before I knew it, he was quiet and back asleep. He was so spoiled because he knew I would pick him up and hold him.

Holding my little brother in my arms made me forget about my mother and Essence pissing

me off. I laid down with him on my chest thinking about how uncorrupted he was. He couldn't
disappoint me or let me down. He made me
appreciate the little things in life.

After I put Michael back in his bassinet, I got
on the computer and continued my search for
an agent. Lord knows I needed something else
to focus on.

May

"What's up with you and Essence?" Paul asked me as he weaved his truck in and out of traffic.

"A bunch of bullshit. She won't let me hit. My balls couldn't be any bluer," I admitted.

He laughed at me. "Are you serious, bro?"

"As a heart attack."

"How come she won't let you hit? She waiting for marriage or something?" he cracked on me.

"Beats the hell out of me. I been doing everything to show her I'm interested. Apparently, that's not good enough. I'm not going to keep playing myself, though. Either she's going to come around, or I'm moving on." I sounded tough, but on the inside, I hoped like hell she came around. I couldn't look soft in front of Paul, though.

"Communication is the key to everything. Remember that. Be up front about your feelings. If you just want to smash, then say that. If you want a relationship with her, then say that. Be as direct as possible. She can't deny the truth."

I became suspicious when Paul pulled up in front of Essence's house.

"I thought we were going to play ball."

"I can see it in your eyes that she means something to you. I don't want you to blow your opportunity. Trust me, you'll thank me for this later."

"I can't just show up to her place unannounced."

"Stop stalling, bro," Paul said and smiled. "You good."

I sighed. "Here goes nothing," I said and got out of the truck.

We fist-bumped through the window.

"Be direct and up front about your feelings. You can't go wrong, bro."

"I got you."

"Later."

Paul pulled off, and I felt jittery as I got closer to her front door. Before I could ring the doorbell, she answered the door dressed in a pair of tight blue jeans and a revealing blouse. She was beautiful.

"What do you want?" Essence asked with her hand on her hip and her neck craned to the side.

"I want us to start over. We got off on the wrong foot the other night."

She sighed and waved me inside the house.

Essence sat on the couch, and I went into the kitchen and got a soda. I noticed the trash was full, so I took the bag outside. When I came back in, I slouched back on the couch and put my feet on the coffee table.

"The way you left out of here was childish." She crossed her arms.

"I'm sorry. I was frustrated. I like you a lot, and I have no idea how you feel about me."

"I enjoy hanging out with you and everything, but I'm not ready for us to have a relationship."

"We don't have to be together to have sex, Essence. Stop trying to play me."

"If I give you some, I'm sure you'll want to be with me," she said cockily.

"Aren't we full of ourselves?" I said.

"All I'm saying is don't expect us to be together if we have sex."

"I won't," I said nonchalantly.

"Okay," she said with a sly smile and slid on top of me. She kissed me on my neck, chin, and lips. I became hard beneath her. Not knowing what the hell to do, I froze up and let her take the lead.

She unzipped my pants and took off her blouse and bra. Next, she stood and removed her jeans and panties. Following her lead, I stood and got naked too.

Seeing her naked for the first time up close, I almost exploded. She had light brown nipples, a little gut, and she didn't have any hair down there like the girls I watched on porn.

When we kissed, she caught me off guard because she used her tongue this time. It took me a minute to get in sync with her. I grabbed her ass with both hands. Her skin was so soft.

Wanting to hurry the process along, I abandoned the kiss, and we rushed upstairs holding hands.

"Grab a condom out of the nightstand," she told me when we got into the bedroom. The anticipation had me on edge.

Damn, how many guys have you been with? I thought and then focused on finding a condom. I searched through the nightstand drawer, grabbed one, and ran into the bathroom.

Sweat poured from my forehead as I tried to get the condom on right. Then I heard a popping sound. When I looked down, the condom had a hole in it.

"Shit!" I yelled.

"Everything okay in there?"

I went back into the bedroom feeling like an idiot. "I need another condom."

She looked down at my crotch and laughed. "Come here and let me help you, boy."

I looked at the ceiling while she put another condom on me.

She pushed me on the bed and hopped on top of me. She guided me into her warm moistness with little effort. I saw stars and a kaleidoscope of different colors when I slipped inside of her.

She rode me like a professional jockey and grabbed me by the shoulders forcefully.

"Wait . . . wait!" I yelled and tried to warn her. She stopped when she felt me shake and become stiff under her. I closed my eyes and bit my lip to keep from yelling. I had never done drugs before, but I'm sure sex had the same effect on you.

"Wow. Really, Anthony?" She sucked her teeth, pulled the cover over her, and turned to the wall. "I can't believe I wasted my damn time with you."

I had never been more embarrassed in my life.

June

Essence and I didn't speak for three weeks after the first time we had sex. I was too embarrassed to call her. I'm sure she didn't want to speak to me either.

On the flip side, I desperately wanted another chance to prove myself to her in the bedroom. Our situation got off to a rough start, and I wanted to rectify things if I could.

In those three weeks, we didn't speak, I Googled "better sex habits." Surprisingly, I found some good things I could use the next time we were intimate with each other. Everything from setting the mood to kissing to timing. I could've easily asked Paul, but I didn't want to go there with him. Best friend or not, this was a touchy subject for me to speak about.

Feeling like I was ready to win Essence over, I went to a flower shop near her house and bought a bouquet of long stemmed roses. The woman behind the counter said there isn't a better way to say, "I'm sorry." I couldn't have agreed more.

After I got off the bus and walked a couple of blocks, I stood at Essence's front door. I took a deep breath and rang her doorbell. After a few minutes, I heard footsteps nearing the door. I cleared my throat and smiled.

"Something I can help you with, boss?" A brown-skinned man with no shirt on asked me.

I almost hit him in the head with the flowers. "Who the hell are you?"

"Look, boss, let me go and get Essence right quick." He closed the door in my face. My face got hot, and I kept tapping my foot. I wanted this dude to come outside so I could knock his head off.

Essence and the unknown man argued with each other before the door flew open, and the man brushed by me and got into his black BMW.

"Who was that?" I asked as she let me into the house.

"He's an old boyfriend," she said nonchalantly. "His name is Austin."

"An old boyfriend, huh? Are there any other *old boyfriends* I should know about who might just stop by your house?" I asked suspiciously.

"Slow your roll, Anthony. You and I aren't together. I don't report to you," she said with much attitude.

"I understand all that, but I didn't know you slept around that much."

"It's not like you're off to a good start in the sex department. Shit, I need to get it from somewhere."

My stomach went sour at the thought of another man inside of her.

"Look, I came to apologize about that, and I bought you these." I handed her the roses. She gave me a half smile and put them in the kitchen inside a pitcher of water.

"How come you haven't called me?" she folded her arms across her chest.

"I was embarrassed, and to be honest, I didn't know how to come at you." It felt good to get that off my chest.

"This whole time I wanted you to call me, but I should've been the one who called you. Everybody has a bad day. It's not like it was your first time or anything," she reasoned with me.

She looked at me confused when I didn't say anything back to her.

"Wait a minute. You were a virgin?" Her mouth hung wide open.

I looked at the ground. "I was one until about three weeks ago."

"No wonder you lasted two damn minutes. At least you could've gave me the heads-up." She threw her arms in the air and crushed my ego.

"I want to make up for the other night." I stepped closer to her. Invading her space felt good, and I had no idea where this wave of confidence came from.

"Anthony, you don't have—" she began.

I pressed my lips against hers so she would shut up. As we kissed, I slowly rubbed on her breasts and nipples. When she wrapped her arms around me, I cupped her ass. The scent of her perfume made me breathe harder.

She broke the kiss and told me, "Take your clothes off now."

I quickly did as I was told, and she got undressed too.

We walked up the steps holding hands. Once we got into her bedroom, I grabbed a condom out of the drawer and went into the bathroom.

Taking my time, I slowly put the condom on successfully and went back into the bedroom like a man on a mission.

After a few minutes of licking everywhere between her thighs, I laid her down on the bed and guided myself into her wetness with little effort. I kissed on her neck and cheek, and she moaned with approval. I felt like the man.

Keeping my pace even and my mind on not coming too fast again, I stroked her slowly. I rotated my hips clockwise, and then counter-clockwise. I hit spots she didn't even know were there.

"Yes, boy. *That's* how you please mama," she said and slapped me on the ass to encourage me to go harder.

I increased my speed when she slapped me.

"Yes. Faster!" she yelled.

The sound of our skin smacking together echoed throughout the room and sweat poured from my forehead.

My body shook from a forceful orgasm, and I bit my lip to keep from yelling. Essence kissed me on the forehead and got out of bed. She came back with a washrag and cleaned me and herself off.

I had no idea what cuddling was until Essence told me to hold her that night. Lying there, I thought about how my mother wanted me to be with someone younger than Essence. Although my mother cared about Essence's age, I didn't. I had feelings for her, and I wanted to explore them.

Because we had sex, I felt like I could open up my soul to her. "Can I ask you a question?"

"Of course."

"Are your parents together?"

"No. My father left us," she said coldly.

"Mine did too."

"What made you think of him?"

"My mother thinks you'll take advantage of me like my father did to her because of their age difference."

"That's very presumptuous," she huffed.

I smiled. "Tell me about it."

"Did you blame yourself for him leaving?"

"I did, and I don't know why."

"I don't know why I did either."

"How do you deal with him not being there?"

"My stepfather stepped up in his absence."

"Would you ever accept your biological father back in your life?" I asked.

She smiled. "Never say never."

"Did you ever find out why he left or where he is?"

"To be honest, I don't want to know."

"I want to know where my dad is. I miss him, and I want him to come back home." I let the tears fall.

She wiped my tears away with her thumb.

I hugged her tighter, and within minutes, I was sleeping.

I woke up a few hours later to an empty bed. I grabbed my cell phone off the nightstand, and I had a text message from Essence.

I had some business to take care of. I'll call you later.

After I yawned and stretched, I got out of the bed, took a birdbath, and put my clothes back on.

Curiosity got the best of me, and I went through her medicine cabinet. I found some codeine tablets prescribed to her ex-boyfriend, Austin, and I took a picture of the pill bottle with my cell phone. Something told me the picture of his address on the pill bottle would come in handy someday.

I caught the bus home and decided to smooth things over with my mother. During the last three weeks, we spoke to each other, but we didn't directly address our issues.

I came in the house, and my mother was in the living room watching *Family Feud*.

"Anthony," she said and didn't look at me.

"Mom." I matched her tone. I took a deep breath and continued on. "I wanted to apologize for the way I acted. Dealing with women is a new thing for me. I just want your support, that's all."

"Come here and sit down." She patted the space beside her on the couch.

I did as I was told.

"You'll always have my support. Unfortunately, I don't want you to be with an older woman. You get with someone your own age, and I'm all in."

"Why does age matter so much to you?"

"I don't want to see you get hurt or taken advantage of because of your inexperience. Senior used my naivety to deceive me," she revealed.

"I told you I can handle myself. I'm more mature than you think I am."

She shook her head. "I don't tell you to do things because I'm perfect. It's because I've been where you are. I've felt what you're feeling. Your emotions are all over the place. I get that."

I let my guard down. "We're in a gray area right now. More than friends, but not officially in a relationship."

"That's okay right now. Relationships aren't something to rush into. Let things happen naturally."

"If we do pursue a relationship, do you think you'll ever warm up to her?" I asked.

"I can't promise you anything."

"That's better than no," I said and smiled.

She smiled back and hugged me.

"It's my job to protect you. You may not like what I say, but I have good intentions."

"I know you do."

After my mother went out, I put Michael down for the night. Then I called Paul on his cell phone.

"What's up, bro?" he asked.

"Nothing much. What's up with you?"

"Chillin'. I was watching *CSI* reruns."

"Guess what happened?"

"What?"

"Essence let me hit again."

"Are you serious, bro?"

"Dead serious."

"I thought she wouldn't let you near her after what happened the first time."

"Me too."

"How you feeling about her now."

"I just want to see where things go from here."

"The great thing is you don't have to rush. Just let things happen organically. You'll figure out what to do."

September

Sex with Essence became addictive. Sometimes that's all I could focus on. I spent at least two nights out of the week at her house cooking, cleaning, or having sex with her. Despite all of this, we still didn't have a title, and we had been dealing with each other for a minute. Something had to give.

In my heart, I felt like we were a couple. Pretending that we weren't would be stupid. The bottom line was I wanted us to be together.

Once I got back to her house after work, she came to the door wearing one of my T-shirts. Her nipples strained against the thin fabric. I could tell she just stepped out of the shower because her hair was still wet. I pulled her into a French kiss and rubbed on her ass.

She broke the lip-lock between us and removed her shirt. I followed behind her into the dining room like an obedient puppy.

"Have a seat. I'll have dinner ready in a minute," she said. Art of Noise's "Moments in Love" played from her cell phone on the dining-room table. She set the mood perfectly.

With lust on my mind and an empty stomach, I sat at the table horny and hungry. I didn't know if I wanted to taste her first or what she made for dinner.

Seeing her stand at the stove with no clothes on almost made me get up from the table and jump her bones. Patience and I weren't the best of friends, but I damn sure waited on her.

Fifteen minutes later, she set a plate of food in front of me. She made us gorgonzola-stuffed pork chops, sautéed garlic asparagus, and Spanish rice.

She pulled out a bottle of red wine for the occasion.

"One or two glasses won't hurt you." She opened the bottle and poured us each a glass of wine.

After we finished dinner and the entire bottle of wine, we went to the bedroom. The buzz I had from the wine didn't prevent me from noticing the rose petals scattered all over the bed or the massage oil on the nightstand.

"I wanted to try something new," she said with a mischievous grin.

"Cool. I'm wit' it." I rubbed my hands together in anticipation.

We rubbed massage oil on each other's bodies. The foreplay became intense as we licked each other all over with no limitations.

We tried to one-up each other. I pulled her hair, and she bit my neck. I pulled on her nipples, and she grabbed my balls. I bit her ass, and she choked me. She even slapped me across the face. I egged her on to slap me again, and she did. We played sexual ping-pong.

I discovered I enjoyed when she hit me. Maybe not on a regular basis, but definitely some of the time when we had sex. She pulled the freak out of me.

She pinned me down by the wrists and rode me like a wild woman. "This is how you wanted it, didn't you?" she whispered in my ear.

I nodded like a small child. She swiveled her hips like a porn star. She tightened her grip on my wrists; I knew she was close to an orgasm. So was I. Minutes later, we came together.

"Damn, girl. What are you trying to do to me?" I asked, exhausted from our sexual workout.

"I'm sorry for unleashing the freak on you."

"No, you're not!" I hit her on the shoulder lightly.

Around 2:00 a.m., I woke up out of my sleep, and Essence was almost nose to nose with me. She scared the hell out of me.

"Anthony, can I ask you a question?" she whispered.

"Sure, anything. What's on your mind?" I yawned and stretched. I wouldn't have minded going another round with her.

"We like each other, right?" She sounded unsure.

"Yes. Of course, we do." I liked where this was headed.

"And this is going somewhere, right?"

"Absolutely."

"Come and live with me then." She half-smiled.

I jumped out of the bed, hit the lamp switch, and circled around the bedroom. I thought she wanted us to be together. She went totally left.

"You're sending me mixed messages," I said. "I thought you said we were just messing around with each other. You said you weren't looking for anything serious, and at the time, I agreed with you. Now you want us to live together, just like that?" I snapped my fingers to emphasize my point. "We aren't even together."

"I want us to be together," she said and grabbed my hand.

I softened my stance a bit. "I want us to be together too, but moving in is a huge decision for us to make."

"I need you next to me every night. I hate when you have to leave and go home. Don't you?" she pleaded with me through her eyes.

"Can I think about it and get back to you?"

"I'm offering you a piece of my life, and you ask me can you think about it? Maybe we don't have the connection I thought we had." She roughly pulled the covers over herself and turned away from me.

I walked over to the other side of the bed so I could look into her eyes. "That's not true. We most definitely have a connection with each other."

"Sounds like all I am to you is a booty call." I could've sworn I saw tears in her eyes. Seeing she was hurt, I tried to console her.

"Don't touch me! I can't believe how selfish you are." She yelled and left me standing there looking stupid.

Feeling like shit, I put my clothes back on and called an Uber. Once the Uber pulled up to her house, I hopped in. I wanted to be with Essence, and obviously, she wanted to be with me too, but I wanted my own apartment. I had to find a way to tell her that without hurting her feelings.

Easier said than done.

I also didn't want to seem like I was abandoning my mother and Michael. It was a lot to think about. I couldn't wait to go home and get drunk.

When we got to my block, I paid the Uber driver and went in the house and straight to the kitchen. I took several shots of vodka to calm my nerves.

Before I knew it, I had drunk enough vodka to convince myself to at least consider moving in with Essence . . . although moving out meant I would be leaving my mother and little brother behind.

Maybe it was time to leave the nest.

Maybe it wasn't.

Only time would tell if I was right.

September

I drowned myself in vodka again the next afternoon to build up the confidence to talk to my mother about the possibility of moving in with Essence. To hide the vodka smell, I brushed my teeth three times and gargled with mouthwash.

I sat down at the dining-room table with my mother. "I wanted to run something by you," I said and sipped iced tea.

"Go ahead. I'm listening."

"What do you think about me moving out of here?"

She smiled. "I think that's great. You either found a place or you're looking for one, right?"

"Not exactly."

"What do you mean not exactly?" she asked and made air quotes.

"Essence and I are becoming serious and—"

She cut me off. "And she thinks you should move in with her."

I swallowed hard. "Yes."

"Wow. She thinks for you too," she said sarcastically.

I closed my eyes and rubbed my forehead. "Essence and I will be together. At this point, I don't care if you approve. I was just asking your opinion as a courtesy. I haven't made up my mind yet anyway."

She leaned back in her chair and smirked. "I guess you got it all figured out, huh?"

"No. I don't have it all figured out. I've found somebody that I like a lot, and my mother refuses to be happy for me."

"The bottom line is, she's too old for you. Why can't you see that?"

"Your age excuse is getting really old. You need to focus on something else." I slapped the table.

"Having a relationship with an older woman is one thing. Moving in with her will be much worse. If you make this decision, and it fails, don't say I didn't warn you."

"I'm eighteen years old now. I'll be the judge if I'm making a bad decision."

"*Excuse* me? Repeat what you said. I didn't understand you." She cupped her ear.

"You heard me," I said defiantly.

"So now you're grown all of a sudden? You could've fooled me."

"Yes, I'm grown. I don't ask you for anything, and I pay my own way around here."

She clapped. "Welcome to adulthood. You don't get an award for paying your bills. If you want to be real, you aren't doing much."

With anger blinding my vision, I jumped out of my seat and stood in her face. Anger bubbled inside of me like a pot of boiling water.

"This isn't about Essence's age. This is about you needing help with Michael. He's *not* my son. He's my *little brother*. It would be wise of you to remember that."

"You can be so damn selfish sometimes, just like your father."

Her words jabbed at me like a knife. Obviously, she enjoyed pushing my buttons.

My eyes grew wide. "I'll make this easy for both of us. I'm out of here."

She looked disappointed, and I couldn't have cared less.

As I stormed out the door, I heard her talking, but I ignored what she said. When I got outside, I called Paul on his cell phone.

"What's up, bro?"

"I had a fight with my mom, and I need to get out of here."

"You wanna hit up Dave & Buster's?"

My face lit up like Christmas lights. "Hell yeah."

"I'm on my way."

I hated being at odds with my mother, but in my eyes, she continued to play me. If she wanted to be a jackass, I could be one too. Going out to Dave & Buster's would give me the distraction I desperately needed.

When Paul pulled up on me, I hopped in the truck, and we shook hands.

"Now I can bust your ass again in basketball," I said as Paul pulled off.

Paul smirked. "Not a snowball's chance in hell, bro."

My cell phone buzzed in my pocket. It was a text message from Essence.

Until you can make a decision on moving in with me, don't expect us to have sex.

September

I didn't respond to Essence's text message. The fact that she tried to use sex to force me into a decision disappointed me. I refused to communicate with her or my mother.

Feeling aggravated, I got caught up in a vicious cycle of sleepwalking through work, and then coming home and getting wasted. Waffling between staying at my mother's house, getting my own apartment, and moving in with Essence made me hit the bottle harder.

I also wanted my mother to respect my decision-making skills. She had a responsibility to protect me, but she also had to know the right time to let go. This was that time.

The only positive to come out of the situation was that I amped up my efforts to get my screenplays noticed. I bought ad space, e-mail lists, and entered my screenplays into a few contests.

Paul offered to let me crash at his place until I figured out what to do next. I took him up on his offer.

Unfortunately, I needed some clothes and stuff, and I had to go to my mother's house to get them. I planned to get in and out of the house without seeing or speaking with her.

I tried to unlock the front door, and for some reason, my key didn't work. I tried several more times before I gave up.

"What the hell is going on?" I said to myself.

The door swung open.

"I had the locks changed," my mother said dryly.

I shrugged. "No problem. I just came by to get some of my stuff anyways. I'll be out of your way in a minute."

She followed me upstairs. "So, you don't have anything to say to me?"

"Nope." I went into my bedroom to get some books and clothes. I was tired of wearing Paul's stuff.

"Anthony, we really need to talk."

I turned and faced her after I put my things in an old book bag. "About what? You made your point very clear the last time we talked."

"I understand you're growing, but it's my job to give you the best advice I can."

"What if the advice is wrong? You ever think of that?"

"I'm two minutes from popping you in your smart-assed mouth."

"Do you wanna fight me, Mom? Will that make you feel better?" I asked, my arms out wide.

"If you could stop being so damn stubborn that would make me feel better."

"I have to make the best decision for me. Whatever that is."

She caressed my face lovingly. "I don't want you to have any regrets."

I pulled away from her and scowled. "I won't."

"I really hope not."

I walked back downstairs to the front door. She followed me.

"I just want what's best for you."

"I know." I didn't bother turning around to face her.

"I don't want you to go."

"I'm sorry, Mom. I have to." I put my hand on the doorknob.

"Don't do this because you're mad at me," she said and let the tears fall.

"I'm not." I turned around and hugged her before I left the house.

My phone went off when I got outside. Essence's name popped up on the caller ID. I thought about ignoring the call but then decided against it. If I wanted a future with this woman, I couldn't ignore her forever. Something had to give.

She went right in. "Can I ask you a question?"

"Sure," I said and played along.

"What are we?"

"I thought we were just kicking it with each other."

"So we aren't a couple?"

"I don't know. You tell me."

"I would like us to be a couple."

I couldn't help but smile.

"I feel the same way."

"And I'm sorry for giving you a sex ultimatum."

"It's water under the bridge now."

Just like that, we were official, and man, did it feel good. I realized in the moment how stupid it was for us to not be speaking.

"I won't pressure you into moving in with me, though. Either you want to or don't."

"I don't have a problem moving in with you. I just always wanted a place to call my own."

"I been there, so I totally understand. I do think I can persuade you to come and live with me."

"How so?" She piqued my interest.

"I'm lying here in the bed naked. Won't you come over here and find out?"

I felt my manhood swell. "I'll be there as soon as I can." I ended the call.

I needed to find out how persuasive Essence could be.

October

After debating with myself, and then having another long discussion with Essence, I decided to move in with her. She sold me on how much money I would save by splitting the mortgage with her instead paying rent by myself. Paying five hundred a month instead of a thousand was a no-brainer. She also encouraged me to use the extra money to further my film career, and that endeared me to her.

I always had my mother to lean on, and now I had to build a solid foundation with Essence. The opportunity excited me. Being able to have sex with Essence anytime I wanted to didn't hurt either.

"Anthony," Paul yelled from the living room.

"What's up?" I asked as I stood in the bathroom mirror.

"Essence is calling you on your phone."

"Okay." I splashed water on my face and then patted it dry with a hand towel.

I went into the living room and sent Essence a text message.

She sent me a text back saying she would be at Paul's apartment in five or ten minutes.

"You sure about moving in with her?" Paul asked. He sounded uncertain.

"I'm 100 percent sure."

"I hope you're right, bro."

"You think I'm crazy, don't you?"

"I don't think you're crazy. I think moving in with her is premature."

"How so?"

"When two people aren't on even ground, that can create problems. Be careful. That's all I'm saying."

"I hear you."

My phone vibrated with another text message from Essence.

"She's downstairs," I said and grabbed my bag.

By the time Paul and I got outside, she hopped out of her truck.

"It's nice to meet you, Paul," she said and shook his hand.

"Nice to meet you too. Make sure you treat my boy right."

"I will," she smiled politely.

I held her by the waist and kissed her on the lips. "Give me a minute, and I'll be right there."

"Okay." She got back into the truck.

"Thank you for opening up your place to me." I gave Paul dap and a hug.

"No problem, bro. You just be careful like I told you. And if things don't work out, my door is always open."

Truth be told, nervousness swirled around my stomach. I wanted my independence, but deep down, I wanted to prove my mother wrong too.

It was time to shit or get off the pot.

December

After two months of living together, Essence and I were still getting along okay, but my money was tight, and I could see this becoming a problem if I didn't find a better-paying job.

Once we split the bills, I rarely had any money left over for myself. The last time we went out to dinner, I ordered water and the cheapest entrée on the menu. I couldn't take being broke much longer.

On top of that, I still couldn't get an agent's attention. My frustration level was on ten, but I was determined to better my situation.

This particular night, Essence sat at the dining-room table number crunching, and I sat next to her on her laptop researching job opportunities and editing a new screenplay.

Every time she hit a button on the calculator, I became more worried about our financial situation. The money flew out of my bank account into someone else's bank account. These were the pitfalls of adulthood, I guess.

She turned around in her seat. "Anthony, we agreed to split the bills fifty-fifty. Right now, your portion feels kind of light."

I scrunched up my face and closed the laptop. "I give you everything I have. Ninety percent of my paycheck goes to bills and household needs. You know that already."

She ignored my comment.

"I pay the majority of the bills, and that has to change, or we need to reevaluate some things in our relationship."

I felt threatened by her statement.

"I don't say shit when you splurge on $300 purses or shoes," I countered and folded my arms across my chest.

She shook her head. "Men step up to the plate. Boys make excuses. Which one are you?"

I stood. "I'm a grown-ass man. I'll get another job or do some OT. Don't act like I'm slacking or something. I do my part around here without hesitation."

"Obviously, you're not doing your part as good as you think you are." She stood too.

"Whatever, I'm out of here." I waved her off dismissively.

"Go ahead and run away like a little boy."

I grabbed my keys and jacket and left the house.

The fresh air against my face felt good. Essence and I arguing over money wasn't a part of my plan. This shit had to stop.

In the beginning, she did any and everything in the bedroom, and now she was in the mood every once in a while. When she knew she had me, she stopped putting forth the energy needed to sustain our relationship.

She knew I barely had enough to pay my portion of the bills and let me know every chance she got.

Things were falling apart.

I took the bus to Center City and went into Wine and Spirits. I scanned the shelves and found a bottle of vodka. Even though I didn't get carded, I was still on edge.

Luckily for me, there was a pretty woman at the register. A quick smile and a little flirtation got me out of the store without any problems.

Barnes & Noble was two blocks away and just being outside was good enough for me.

The bright lights of Center City at night always fascinated me.

Once I got to the bookstore, I ordered a latte and went to the bathroom. Inside the stall, I poured vodka into the latte and went back out to the main floor.

I found a quiet spot to sit on the floor between the magazine section and a bookshelf. Observing people always gave me interesting material to write about. There was a mix of college kids and business types in the store. I wondered what their problems were and if they were masking them. Their facial expressions, clothing choices, and what came out of their mouths made for good description and dialogue. Sometimes the material wrote itself.

I stayed at Barnes & Noble until 10:45 p.m. typing screenplay ideas into my cell phone memo pad. By that time I had polished off two vodka lattes. I lumbered outside and caught the bus back home.

Back at the house, I crept up the steps and peeked into our bedroom and Essence was snoring.

I went downstairs and plopped down on the couch in the living room.

I needed more money, and Essence was showing me how impatient she could be. In my heart, I felt like we could get past this, but it had to be a joint effort.

I didn't need her to compound the problem by telling me how little money I contributed. I needed her full-fledged support if we were going to make it through this rough patch.

December

On a Sunday afternoon, Essence and I sat at a table in the café at Barnes & Noble. She read one of those "100 Ways to Improve Your Life" articles in a women's magazine while I e-mailed my pitch letter around to various agents while also looking for another job.

On the way to the bathroom, I passed a community information board. Someone had put up a flyer advertising a contest for writers, and the details interested me. First place in the contest received $1,000. Second place received $750. Third place received $225.

The top three candidates in the contest could win the money and a possible pitching session with a movie studio executive. I took the informational flyer and went back to our table. The excitement of the opportunity bubbled inside of me as I sat back down. The last few writing contests that I entered weren't fruitful, so I needed this one to work.

"You and Paul still hanging out tonight?" Essence asked me without looking up from her magazine.

"Of course," I said flatly.

"Funny how you have time to bowl, but you can't work any overtime at your damn job."

"I've begged my boss for more work. Nothing's available right now. I can't make them give me time that's not available." I closed the laptop and focused my attention on Essence.

"I'm sick of not having money because I have to cover for you too. I didn't sign up for this."

I slumped my shoulders. "I've been looking for jobs. I can't force people to hire me. I'm doing the best I fucking can." I pounded my hand on the table and got a couple of funny looks.

"How hard have you really been looking?"

"I'm on Indeed and CareerBuilder every day, so stop talking out of your ass."

"If you've been looking so hard, how come you haven't found anything yet?" she countered.

I shook my head. "Because nothing happens overnight. Things take time. When the right opportunity comes along, I'll be all over it."

With her lips pursed and her eyes narrowed, she said, "You need to speed up the process."

***

Later that same evening, Paul and I were on our second game of bowling at Lucky Strike in Center City. We ate mozzarella sticks, soft pretzel nuggets, and talked shit with each other. I desperately needed a guy's night out.

"Essence is pissed because I don't make as much money as she does."

"What's your game plan to bring in more money, bro?" Paul went into his bowling stance.

"I'm going to do some OT when it becomes available and hopefully find another job. I've been looking for one since I moved in with her. I can't find anything, and it's frustrating," I sighed.

Paul flung the bowling ball down the lane and hit four pins.

"She should be happy you have a job and you're trying to find another one."

"She won't be happy until I get one."

"Something will come along. I can feel it." He came to the table and patted me on the shoulder. "Women want security. That's a part of the game. You gotta know that going in."

"I know, and I want to give her security. I gotta get on solid ground first, though."

"I have faith in you, bro." Paul nearly had a spare.

On my next turn, I threw a gutter ball. I hoped it wasn't a sign of things to come.

December

Some mornings I tried to kiss Essence on the lips, and she moved her face, so I caught her on the cheek. I wanted us to be in a better space, but she was content to have us in turmoil. Sometimes I didn't understand her.

I went out of my way to cook more and try to set the mood, and Essence blocked all of my attempts. In my heart, I knew that her attitude wouldn't change until I brought in some more income.

I turned into a dollar sign instead of a boyfriend. She could've been encouraging, but she talked down to me and became argumentative.

After I poured myself a cup of coffee spiked with vodka, I logged on to the screenwriting contest's Web site and submitted my screenplay named *Compromised*.

As I thought of Essence and our relationship problems, my mother popped into my head. I could see her saying moving in with Essence was a mistake, and I needed to be with a younger woman. All I wanted to do was make her proud. I wanted to show her that I could stand on my own two feet. My method of telling her was way off, but in the moment, I let my emotions get the best of me, and I shouldn't have.

We definitely needed to talk, and there was no time like the present. I called her house phone and prayed that she picked up.

She went right in on me when she answered the phone.

"You have a lot of nerve calling me. What do you want?" she sounded agitated.

I took a deep breath. "I'm sorry, Mom, for the way I spoke to you. I had to show you I could do things on my own."

"I know you can be independent. You've always been self-sufficient. I just wanted to prepare you for this relationship. Women aren't easy to deal with. I know because I'm not always easy to deal with my damn self."

"I never imagined living here would be this hard."

She laughed. "Let me guess. You thought you were going to give up a little money and she would give you all the sex you wanted, right?"

"Maybe not exactly that way, but close." I couldn't help but laugh.

"I'm not thrilled about you guys living together or being together, but I can learn to accept your decision. You're grown now, I can respect that."

"I'm glad to hear that. It means a lot coming from you."

"I love you, son, and I want you to be happy."

"I love you too, Mom."

"You just be careful and value the relationship."

"I will."

"Things will get tough, but how you handle it says a lot about the man you are or the man you're not."

"I know," I sighed.

"Trust me, everything will be okay. It takes time to get used to living with each other."

When I got off the phone with my mother, I felt better about my living situation.

Not to mention she made a great point about being patient.

Later that day at work, I loaded the dishwasher and ran the silverware through a wash, rinse, and drying cycle. The restaurant was abuzz with activity, and the kitchen area was chaotic.

I cleared the empty tables and took the bin of dirty dishes to the precleaning area. I had to repeat this process at least fifteen to twenty times a day. It annoyed the hell out of me.

"Anthony, when you're done with what you're doing, come to my office so we can talk," Phaedra said to me. Her tone didn't reveal her mood. Not a good sign. I was scared, and my breathing became labored.

With nervous energy flowing through me, I dried my hands off with a dish towel and threw the rag into the dirty linen pile. I walked into her office and forced a smile. She motioned for me to sit down in the chair in front of her. I did as I was told.

"Anthony, you've been one of the most consistent employees during your tenure here." She paused.

My hands wouldn't stop shaking. I couldn't come up with a reason for me to be fired. Nothing stood out, and the uncertainty of the situation sent me into a panic. As far as I knew, I did everything I was supposed to.

"I hate this part of being a supervisor. I truly do. Unfortunately, I have to cut everybody's hours for the foreseeable future. Business is trending downward, and this is a temporary solution to shave our money losses. This is not an indictment against you or your work ethic. You've done everything required of you and more. I thank you for your commitment."

She offered a warm smile and an understanding tilt of the head. I had been dropped into the pressure cooker. Beads of sweat formed on me almost everywhere at once. Images of Essence's face all twisted up in anger haunted me. As soon as I told her the bad news, I could imagine her giving me an earful about it. I dreaded even going home. I could smell the liquor because I wanted a taste so bad.

"I totally understand." I nodded and half-smiled. "How many hours am I losing?" I slouched back in the chair.

"You'll lose one shift per week."

"I hope things pick up soon."

"Me too."

The rest of the day blurred together for me, and I walked around like one of the zombies from Michael Jackson's *Thriller* video. After I got off work, I called Essence on her cell phone to see what kind of mood she was in.

"I'll be over at Paul's apartment for a few hours."

Paul pulled up to the front of my job. I got in the passenger side of his truck and gave him a handshake.

"Again? He your girlfriend now?" she asked sarcastically.

Great. She was in a shitty mood.

"Man, you're seriously tripping."

"Let me know if I should be scared you're going to leave me and be with him."

"You can kiss my ass," I yelled and pounded my fist on the dashboard. "And another thi—"

She disconnected the call before I could finish.

"Was that Essence?" Paul asked.

"How could you tell?" I asked sarcastically.

"Pure luck," he said, and we laughed.

We got to Paul's University City apartment in no time. I was just glad to be anywhere but home.

I flopped down on his brown couch.

"What's up with you?" Paul asked. "You were quiet most of the ride over here."

"I'm losing hours at my job. Everything is falling apart." I rubbed my forehead.

Paul sat down on the couch with me and patted me on the shoulder. "I'm sorry, man. You know if you need to borrow some money all you gotta do is ask, bro."

"I appreciate it, man, but I wouldn't put you in that position."

He waved me off. "You're like my brother. Whatever is mine is yours. You know that."

"I feel like I'm cursed. The more I try to do right, the more shit goes wrong."

"At this point, all you can do is look for a part-time gig and come at Essence with the truth."

I gave Paul the side eye. "I don't think telling Essence my hours got cut is the best idea. She's already pissed off with me."

"If you don't tell her, shit is only going to get worse, bro. Trust me on that." His face became serious.

I looked up at the ceiling. "Maybe you're right."

"You know I'm right."

I couldn't go home and tell Essence I lost hours at my job right away. She would be even more pissed than she already was. I needed to buy some time until I had a better plan to break the news to her.

"You think I can crash here tonight?" I asked.

"No doubt."

"You're a lifesaver."

"You just make sure you handle your business," Paul said, and we shook hands before he went into his bedroom.

I turned the TV on and kicked back on the couch. My feet were on fire from standing all day. Just as I nodded off to sleep my phone vibrated. My mother sent me a text message.

I got a front-office job with the medical aid unit! Just when you least expect it things turn around.

Knowing my mother would be able to make her own money made me happy. But the good news was only a temporary distraction because

I would have to face the music with Essence sooner or later.

Before I went to bed I sent Essence a text message letting her know I wasn't coming home tonight.

She sent me a text back: Tell your girlfriend I said hi.

I tossed my phone on the floor and closed my eyes.

A good night's sleep would do me some good.

December

I was stuck in purgatory. If I told Essence about my reduction in pay, she would probably flip out on me. If I didn't tell her and she noticed the money being lighter, she would flip out on me. Basically, I was fucked.

The next morning, feeling desperate, I found myself standing in The Gallery Mall. Maybe if I gave Essence some gifts when I told her about the lost hours they would soften the blow. I needed to get back on her good side.

I stood frozen inside of Victoria's Secret. I had never been in a lingerie store before, and I swore the workers knew this to be a fact. Being around tight-clothed, big-breasted women selling lingerie made me sweat a little bit. I wanted to touch every store worker's breasts all at the same time.

"Something I can help you with, sir?" a thick, bronze-skinned employee asked me with a sparkling smile.

My mouth watered at the sight of her huge breasts poking out of her top. "Yes . . . uh . . . where is the lingerie section?" I stammered at her visible cleavage.

The awkwardness continued humming right along.

"Follow me," she directed me with a curled finger. I stared at her peach-shaped ass as she walked in front of me.

We stood near a dressed up mannequin and a table covered with lace underwear and bras.

"If you need anything else I'm here to assist you. My name is Sandy." She looked me up and down and licked her lips before walking off.

I bought a red thong, a pair of blue lace crotch-less panties, and a bottle of perfume one of the employees suggested I buy. Before I went back home, I made two more stops in the mall and bought a sterling silver charm bracelet and a piece of gourmet cheesecake. Food and jewelry were a killer combination.

Especially for Essence.

I spent an hour cleaning up the house after I came in from The Gallery. I wiped the baseboards down with an old T-shirt, vacuumed the carpet, and sprayed air freshener. I made sure to put the bag of gifts by the couch. I wanted to set the mood.

Essence walked in the house, and I grabbed her by the waist and kissed her on the lips. She hung her coat in the closet and kicked off her brown high heels. Wanting to make sure she was comfortable, I rubbed her feet when she sat on the couch next to me. I jumped into full pleasure mode.

She gave me the side eye.

She knew something was up.

"Go ahead and tell me the bad news," she said knowingly.

"What? Why would you say that for?" I played dumb.

"Anthony, I'm far from stupid, boy. Men don't voluntarily rub some feet unless something bad happened or they want something in return. Which one is it? Be honest with me."

"That's not true," I said weakly.

"I'm dead tired, boy, and I'm not in the mood to give you some. Just tell me what happened."

I decided to come clean.

"Yesterday my boss told me I'm going to be losing hours." I stared at the ground, hoping for understanding or at least compassion from her.

She moved her foot off my lap.

"I think—" I started to say.

She cut me off. "Your opinion doesn't count for shit right about now. Why haven't you found another job yet? I've been carrying us since you moved in with me. I'm tired of doing every damn thing around here." She slapped the arm of the couch.

"I'm doing the best I can right now. You know this already. Where's all this slick talk coming from?"

"I can't do this alone, boy. Something's got to give. When are you going to start doing more around here?"

"When I get another job."

"And when is that?"

"When I find one!" I yelled.

"Obviously, you're aren't looking hard enough because if you were, you would've found one by now. I'm sorry, but I won't baby you anymore."

I looked at her like she had three heads. "I never asked you to baby me. Instead of bitching at me all the time, how about you be more encouraging? I just told you I'm losing hours at my job, and you keep talking about all of the shit you're doing. The world doesn't revolve around you."

"You got a lot of nerve. You half ass your way around here, and I'm supposed to pat you on your back and say it's going to be okay? Well, it's not going to be okay. We got bills to pay, and you need to come up with a better plan. Clearly, what you're doing now isn't working."

"How is this argument helping us? How does talking down to me get us to where we want to go? Things are tough right now, but I'm going to do my best to turn this situation around. All I can do is try," I said, feeling exhausted.

"I don't *try*. I *do* and I won't let us fall into a deeper hole. I guess I'm built different than you." She went for my ego.

"You know what—" I jumped off the couch and looked down on her.

"What?"

"Nothing. Nothing at all."

"Exactly," she said with a smirk and headed for the stairs, shaking her head. "And a bag of gifts will never make up for a lack of effort on your part." She didn't even bother turning around to face me.

Sitting there on the couch, I was boiling with anger. I had to figure out a way for us to get back into a good space again. Our relationship was on thin ice.

I couldn't take much more of this bullshit.

I looked on the Internet for romantic ideas. I wanted to get Essence's mind off me losing hours at work. Luckily, I was able to book us an affordable hotel suite downtown for Christmas Eve and Christmas Day. Even though I would be losing money, I still wanted to show her I cared about her and this relationship.

Just because we were in a bad spot didn't mean we couldn't still have a good time. Unfortunately, she pouted the entire Uber ride over to the hotel. However, I secured a small win because she agreed to go on the staycation with me and to swap gifts.

The hotel and the gifts I bought stretched my pockets to the limit, but her happiness was priceless. We ordered room service and watched an in-room movie.

"You know that I'm doing everything I can to find a job, right?" I asked as I held her close.

"I do, but the bills are piling up, and our financial situation is getting worse."

I nodded and sighed. "Maybe we can cut the cable off or downgrade the insurance from full coverage to liability."

She laughed. "I'm not cutting my cable off or getting worse insurance because you can't keep up your end of the bargain." She turned away from me and pulled the covers up over her shoulders.

I went to sleep angry because we couldn't even brainstorm together.

Christmas morning we swapped gifts unen-thusiastically with each other, and she couldn't have been colder. I felt like I was banging my head against a brick wall with her.

While she slept later on that night I looked at the snow flurries falling past the window. The scene was so peaceful. I wanted my life to be peaceful too, but it seemed like I couldn't escape the negativity.

Before I went to bed, I prayed to God for our relationship to get on solid ground.

I couldn't take anymore turbulence.

January

After I told Essence about losing hours at work, something shifted in our relationship, and it wasn't for the better. Sometimes she became withdrawn and distant. We went from a little rocky to the *Titanic* against an iceberg.

Most of the time, I drank vodka lattes at Barnes & Noble's café after I got off work and stayed there until they closed. Sometimes on Saturdays and Sundays, I stayed at the bookstore from open to close. I loved how much vodka and lattes went so well together.

Back at work, in the kitchen, I loaded dishes when my phone vibrated inside my pants pocket. I pulled the phone out and checked my e-mail. The writing contest people had sent me a message.

I couldn't find an agent and my relationship with Essence was going to shit, so I needed to hear some good news. With excitement and expectation swirling around in my gut, I ran to the bathroom and read the e-mail.

Dear Mr. Porter,

We are pleased to inform you of your third-place ranking in our annual screenwriting contest. View the attachment for the certificate authenticating the placement. Also remember the screenplay you submitted will be sent to a film executive of our choosing. The studio is under no obligation to respond to us and/or you. All unused materials will be discarded. Thank you for entering the contest, and we wish you much success with your future endeavors.

Later that evening, after I scoured Career-Builder for job opportunities, I sent Paul, Essence, and my mother a text message about the screenwriting contest results. They sent back congratulatory text messages. Although Essence congratulated me, she said she would be happier when I got a better job.

Taking a break from my job search, I figured I could get some writing done. I was so into typing I didn't notice Essence standing over my shoulder.

"So when are you going to wash the dishes and take out the trash?"

"I'll do it when I'm done on the computer."

"You have no sense of urgency," she said and sat down at the table with me.

"I'm not trying to argue with you right now." I rubbed my face and took a deep breath.

"You just don't want to hear the truth." She jabbed her finger in my face.

I scowled and stood. "Man, you better go ahead with that shit."

"Or what you gon' do?" she spat back at me.

I smirked. "You want me to do something stupid, but I won't fall for the banana in the tailpipe. I'm out of here." I grabbed my coat off the chair and stormed out of the house.

Even though it was cold outside, the wind felt good on my face.

I totally understood Essence's frustration about our lack of money, but her smart comments did nothing to propel us forward. I almost felt like she wanted us to be in turmoil just so she would have talking points.

Just as I went to check the Septa bus schedule on my cell phone, a bus slowed to a crawl near the curb.

Once I got inside Paul's building, I knocked on his door. A couple of minutes later, a caramel-skinned woman with long blond-streaked hair and an oversized T-shirt answered the door. Her big nipples strained against her T-shirt. She was bad.

"Can I help you?" she asked.

"I'm Anthony. Is Paul here?"

"Hold on a second," she said and shut the door.

A few moments later, she came back and opened the door. She stepped aside so I could walk in.

"Can you give us a minute?" Paul asked the woman.

"Sure thing," she said and went into the bedroom. I caught a glimpse of her big butt bouncing as she walked away. I smiled and shook my head.

"Another fight with Essence?"

I nodded. "Unfortunately."

The woman came back out fully clothed and kissed Paul on the cheek before she left his apartment.

"I'll call you later, P."

"All right," he said before turning his attention back to me.

"At this point, she's just pissing you off for sport. She wants a reaction. She wants you in a negative space."

"I know, and that's why I came up with a plan during the bus ride over here."

"Anything I can help with?"

I took a deep breath and sat on the couch. "Yeah."

"I need a drink. You want something?" Paul asked as he walked to the kitchen.

"I'll take whatever you have."

A minute later, Paul handed me a glass, and I took a sip.

"This is good, man." The mixed drink left my taste buds tingling.

Paul sat next to me on the couch and took his shot to the head. "It's Grey Goose and lemonade."

"I need me another one," I said.

"Me too."

Paul went back into the kitchen and made us another drink.

"Thanks," I said after accepting the drink.

"What's your plan?"

"I'm going to find us a cheaper insurance carrier, switch our Comcast cable package, and pay off some of our credit cards."

"I hear you. What do you need from me?"

I sighed because desperate times called for desperate measures. This was a desperate time. "I need to borrow a couple of dollars."

"What's a couple of dollars?"

I looked at the ground and said, "A thousand."

"That's it?"

I looked at him confused. "Yeah."

"When my parents died, my aunt Rhonda took me in. Up until I was eighteen, she got money from the state for me. She never spent a dime of it, and on my eighteenth birthday, she gave me a check. I've touched my stash here and there, but I've never made a real dent."

"I can't take that money."

"You can, and you will. Give me your account number, and I'll put it in there in the morning."

Paul was persistent, and he wasn't going to take no for an answer.

I caved in and gave him my banking information.

"I do have a few stipulations, though." Paul smiled devilishly.

I couldn't help but smile too. "I'm listening."

"You're going to volunteer with me at the Boys and Girls Club."

"That's it?" I asked.

"You're also going to help me smash this girl by going on a double date with her ugly friend, bro."

January

I stayed at Paul's house for two days, and all I did was stay on CareerBuilder.com and Indeed.com. My wrists hurt because I typed on the computer so much. Essence and I communicated through text message, and I let her know when I would be home.

I needed a job like yesterday, and I figured with the amount of applications I put in, someone would call me sooner or later.

Paul, being a man of his word, put a thousand dollars in my bank account, and I felt like my plan to get my relationship back on track was bulletproof. All I had to do was put the plan in motion and fill Essence in.

I searched Google for job etiquette feeling like maybe I did something wrong in my interviews. What I found blew me away. I didn't have the right posture, I wasn't asking the right questions, and my appearance needed work.

After I finished searching for jobs on the Internet, I stopped at a discount suit store in Center City. I bought a white shirt, sand-colored slacks, and a nice pair of square-toed shoes. When I tried the clothes on, I felt good. I read somewhere on the Internet when you feel good, you do good. I hoped that was true.

As I was unbuttoning my shirt, my cell phone started buzzing on the wooden bench inside of the dressing room.

I didn't recognize the number, but I picked up anyway.

"Hello," I said sounding unsure.

"Hello. May I speak with Anthony Porter?" a woman asked.

"Speaking."

"Good morning, Anthony. My name is Amanda Caldwell and I'm with Quick Care. I'm calling to see if you were still interested in the front-office position with us," she asked cheerily.

My hands wouldn't stop shaking, and suddenly I couldn't speak.

"Anthony. You still there?" Amanda asked.

"Yes, ma'am. I'm very interested."

"Can you be here in the office in half an hour?"

I looked at the time on my cell phone screen. It was 9:35 a.m.

"Sure thing. I can be there by ten."

"All right, Anthony. We look forward to seeing you soon."

After I paid for my clothes, I hustled to Starbucks and bought me a caramel macchiato. I needed some caffeine in my system.

Luckily for me, Quick Care was only a few blocks away from where I was. I crossed Broad Street and walked until I was standing in front of Quick Care.

There weren't many people in the waiting area so I walked right up to the receptionist.

She smiled warmly before asking, "How can I help you?"

"I'm here for a job interview."

A few minutes later, a thin, brown-haired woman emerged from a set of wooden double doors.

I stood, and we shook hands. "Nice to meet you, Anthony."

"Likewise, ma'am."

"Follow me," she said before using a key card to gain access to the door she came out of.

Amanda gave me a tour of the facility and let me know what my day-to-day duties would be.

To be honest, I was pretty excited about the position. She told me there would be gaps of free time, and all I could think about was time to edit and write new screenplays.

"Do you have any questions for me?"

"No, ma'am. I think you answered everything for me."

"Very well then. We'll see you in a week, sir." She smiled warmly, and we shook hands again.

After I left the job interview, I took the bus to my favorite Barnes & Noble in Center City. Needing a new book to read, I bought the latest Alex Cross hard cover and went outside to catch another bus home.

Something caught my eye. Senior and a woman got out of a silver SUV in front of the TD Bank across the street. At six foot three, the man was hard to miss. He broke my heart when he grabbed a baby from the backseat. From what I could see, the baby had a head full of jet-black curly hair and our same complexion.

I was Senior's first baby boy, and when I saw him with another son, I wanted to strangle him for stepping out on my mother.

That son of a bitch.

They were headed for IHOP, and I bolted across the street and caught him before they could go inside.

The woman with him looked at him funny when she saw me.

"You probably thought you would never see me again, huh?" I said, looking him in the eye.

I wanted him to be uncomfortable, and by the looks of things, I had succeeded.

"Go inside and get us a table, baby. I'll be right in," Senior said to the woman before she and the baby disappeared into the restaurant.

"How are you doing, Junior?" he said like it was nothing.

"How the fuck do you think I'm doing, Anthony?" I crossed my arms. I wanted to be as disrespectful as possible.

"I'm sorry for how things turned out. I never wanted to hurt you and your mother," he said weakly.

I saw this man as a pillar of strength, and here he was, hitting me with this lame bullshit.

I shook my head. "Why did you leave us and start a new family?"

He put his hand on my shoulder. "Your mother and I grew apart, Junior. We had been struggling for years, and I didn't want to fake it anymore."

I saw the sincerity in his eyes, but he still hurt me because of his actions. I pushed his hand off me. "Do you think money solves everything?"

He put his head down. "I know money doesn't solve everything, but I wanted to help you guys out. It's the least I can do."

"How come you didn't call me?" I asked, my voice shaky.

"I was scared. What was I going to say? It became easier to just move on," he admitted.

I felt the tears threatening to come, but I held them back. He wouldn't see me cry. "So me and my mother don't mean shit to you anymore, huh?"

"I will always love you guys, but I have a new family I have to take care of," he said with finality.

My heart turned into a solid block of ice as I smiled at the man with whom I shared almost identical features. I had looked up to this man and wanted to be like him when I grew up. Now, all I saw when I looked at him was disappointment, selfishness, and cowardice.

I became a whirlwind of emotions. All I wanted was Senior to come back home, but he made it clear we weren't a priority in his life anymore. He moved on, and now my mother and I had to move on too. I felt like a piece of garbage, and I promised not to give this man power over me or my emotions anymore.

I hugged him tightly one last time and whispered in his ear, "Fuck you and fuck your new family, motherfucker."

He looked at me in disbelief, and I turned around and walked away from him. I felt the shackles come off.

I would always love my father, but when he chose his new family over my mother and me, he was dead to me. I went and caught the bus home.

I walked in the house and found Essence sitting at the dining-room table looking at a stack of bills.

Not a good sign.

"So you finally brought your black ass home," she said without looking up from what she was doing.

"Nice to see you too, Essence." I went over and sat across from her at the table. "We need to talk about this relationship."

She looked up at me and crossed her arms. "What about it?" The attitude just seeped out of her pores sometimes.

After taking a deep breath, I said, "Where we're going and what we're doing."

"You need to pull your weight around here, and I know you're probably sick of me saying that, but it's the truth."

I touched her hand and surprisingly, she didn't pull away from me. "Look at what I'm wearing."

Her forehead creased in confusion. "What . . . Did you—"

"Yes. I had an interview earlier today," I said proudly.

She smiled so hard I could almost see all of her teeth. "Did you get the job?"

"I start working at Quick Care next week."

She bolted out of her seat and came around and wrapped her arms around me. Her embrace was warm, and she smelled perfect. I inhaled the passion fruit scent she wore. When she touched me, I felt electricity course through me that I hadn't felt in a long time.

"I'm so proud of you," she said in between kisses on my neck, cheek, and lips.

"That means a lot coming from you."

"I want to apologize for the way I acted. I'll do my best to act less bitchy. I promise."

We both laughed.

"In all seriousness, I'm sorry for the times I left the house. We should've been grown enough to talk about our problems instead of sweeping them under the rug."

She sat back down. "You're right. I could've been more supportive. I know you were trying. My frustrations got the best of me, and I was wrong."

"I get frustrated too, but I don't want to make a habit of taking those frustrations out on you. It's not fair to you if I did. I just want us to be happy with each other. That's not asking too much, is it?"

"No. Not at all."

We looked at each other in silence for a few moments.

She got up and kissed me on the mouth. Then she parted my lips with her tongue.

She broke the kiss and said, "Fuck me, Anthony." The urgency in her voice made me hard enough to strain against my dress slacks.

As we kissed some more and groped each other, we made it over to the couch. Once she took off her clothes, I unhooked her bra and pulled her pink lace panties down. I licked and sucked her nipples until she moaned loudly.

I laid her on the couch, and she spread-eagle. On my knees, I feasted on her and sucked her clit until she begged me to stick it in. When I dug into her warmness, she bit my shoulder. After I stroked her slowly, I gave it to her harder, making sure I hit all the right spots.

"Do it faster, baby!" She dug her nails into my back. Our raw skin smacking together and Essence's moans turned me on even more. The harder I went, the louder she screamed my name.

Flipping her over, I pushed her face into the couch and continued to stroke her.

"Just like that, baby!" she screamed.

I grabbed her shoulders and plowed into her until we came together, minutes later. Our foreheads were covered with sweat. Within fifteen minutes, Essence was asleep. She was still beautiful, even with her mouth hanging open and snoring.

Holding her in my arms made everything feel right in my world, and I didn't want to move from that position.

I prayed that this moment snowballed into more sustainability in our relationship.

February

Moving forward, Essence and I strengthened our relationship by spending more time together and getting to *know* each other better.

Moving in together was premature, but necessary to find out our likes and dislikes. Sure, I visited her often. Not often enough to form an accurate opinion on living together, though.

We were common denominators in every problem we had, and we promised to talk things out before they spiraled into an argument. It was easier said than done, but it was a start.

Going out to the movies, eating at expensive restaurants, and spending quality time together made me appreciate what we had. The amount of time we wasted being mad at each other was stupid. I took sole responsibility for my part, and she took responsibility for hers.

I couldn't have been happier.

Our financial situation improved drastically too, because Essence got a raise, and I had two jobs. On top of that, I implemented my plan, and it worked to perfection. With the money Paul gave me, I paid off two credit cards Essence had, we downgraded the cable package, and I found a dirt-cheap insurance carrier. Instead of barely making it to the next payday, we had a little extra money to play with.

At work one day, I stopped off in the break room, and one of my coworkers said the boss was looking for me.

What the hell is going on now?

With slowed footsteps, I went down the hall and knocked on Phaedra's door.

"Come on in," she said from behind her desk.

Phaedra was hunched over a pile of paperwork. Her eyes told a story of being up too late. Even still, she smiled when I sat down. Maybe this was a good sign.

"Good morning, Anthony." Her facial expression went neutral.

"Good morning."

"I'm sad to say that we haven't seen the increase we projected, and I have to cut you back to one-and-a-half shifts per week."

"No problem. Maybe things will turn around in the future," I said and gave her a half smile.

"I hope so. You're a hard worker, and you don't deserve this." We shook hands, and then I left Phaedra's office.

Having a second job eased the pain of losing yet another shift. Something had to give at Phaedra's, though. I couldn't keep playing the guessing game. Either they would give me a steady schedule or I had to move on to greener pastures. I loved working there and respected the hell out of my boss, but they played too many games. I needed a firm commitment from them.

I spent the rest of my shift thinking about how to properly launch my film career. Sure, I had put feelers out for my work, but I needed to step up my efforts to gain visibility.

Later that evening, I walked inside the house. It smelled like garlic butter and rosemary. My stomach rumbled, and I realized I hadn't eaten all day. Seeing Essence standing at the stove, I grabbed her by the waist and kissed her on the neck.

She turned around and kissed me on the mouth. She put her arms around my neck.

The house sparkled, and the food smelled incredible. Damn, I loved this woman.

"How was work?" she asked as she went back to the stove.

I sighed. "Interesting."

"How so?"

"Phaedra cut my hours again."

"Are you serious?"

"Yup. I'm just glad I have Quick Care to lean on."

She adjusted the stove burner and turned and faced me. "We'll be just fine."

"You're right," I said and smiled.

Her vote of confidence calmed me.

She finished at the stove and fixed our plates.

Essence cooked us ribeye steaks, au gratin potatoes, and lemon pepper asparagus.

The steak was fork tender, and every bite of the food was flavorful. We even had a few glasses of red wine.

After dinner, she hit me with something unexpected.

"Since we're in a good financial space, I traded in my truck for a Mercedes-Benz," she said, smiling.

"You got a good deal on the car, right?"

"You know I did. Mama didn't raise no fool."

We high-fived each other.

I didn't mind riding in a Benz. We had a little extra money. Why not?

"Soon as I get my license I'm in there," I said excitedly.

"I don't have a problem with that."

She came around the table and kissed me on the lips. One thing led to another, and Essence and I ended up rolling around on the couch.

After we tired each other out, Essence was snoring up a storm, so I tiptoed downstairs and got on the computer.

I checked the counter at the bottom of my Web site's front page and was disappointed that I only had 292 visitors and no e-mails.

Obviously, the premium marketing I paid for didn't work because that number didn't jump up the way I thought it would. Despite the minor setback, I wasn't deterred.

I dug a little deeper and found various physical addresses for agents located in New York and Los Angeles using Google. The agents in Los Angeles would get personalized letters and gifts, and I would pound the pavement to get the attention of the ones in New York.

I copied and pasted the agencies' addresses into a Word document and printed a copy. Then I purchased a Greyhound bus ticket to New York. This film thing had to work, and I would do whatever was necessary to get into Hollywood's inner circle.

I couldn't wait to go back to the Big Apple.

February

Two days later, I caught the Greyhound bus to the Port Authority in New York City with a messenger bag full of bound screenplays. Once I came out of the building, I smelled roasted peanuts, gyros, and cigarette smoke.

I loved New York ever since I went there for my writer retreat. There was always something interesting to see. Whether it was the theatrics of people on the streets or a landmark you might've seen before somewhere.

The majority of the addresses were in Manhattan, so I jumped into an Uber. During the short ride there I marveled at all the tall buildings and crowded sidewalks.

The Uber driver pulled up to the Avenue of the Arts, and I paid him the fare and climbed out of the car.

The building I needed to be at sat in the middle of the block. I strolled inside and approached the wide wooden, chrome front desk. There was a petite redheaded woman with a bright smile on the telephone. While she talked on the phone, I looked at the list of occupants in the building. Power Play Film Agency was on the fourth floor.

When she got off the phone, she addressed me in a bubbly tone. "How may I help you, sir?"

"I need to speak with someone at Power Play."

Her smile faded, and she took on a look of sadness. "I'm sorry, sir. They don't take unsolicited screenplays."

"I know. Could I give you my screenplay and you pass it along?" I asked with the desperation apparent in my voice.

The woman sighed and looked around before she motioned for me to give her my bound screenplay. "I can't promise you they will contact you, but I can promise I will put this in the hands of the right people."

"Thank you very much," I said and handed her a screenplay out of my messenger bag.

"You're lucky, you're cute," she said and looked me up and down.

I blushed. "I really appreciate this."

I turned around to leave.

"Hold on a sec."

I faced her again. "Yeah?"

"Google a program called Kickstarter so you don't have to put all your eggs in one basket."

I smiled. "I'll look it up. You take care."

"You too."

I gave the attractive woman one last glance before I disappeared out the door.

I visited ten different agencies that afternoon. Six of them let me leave a screenplay without any guarantees that anyone would contact me. Four of them flat out refused to let me leave anything.

I spent the rest of the afternoon mailing screenplays to the Los Angeles agencies and taking in the sights and sounds of New York.

Before I hopped back on the Greyhound bus that night, I visited Nintendo, New York, M&M's world, and ate Hennessy wings at Dallas BBQ in Times Square.

When I got back to Philly, I melted into my bed.

I felt like I was on the right track.

Next week, I got a response from a job that I applied to only a few short weeks ago. I was used to places sending me an automated e-mail turning me down.

I called the number at the bottom of the e-mail, and Emily Waters answered on the second ring.

Emily was the manager at a collection agency. It wasn't the most glamourous position out there, but it would pay the bills, and they had monthly bonus opportunities.

"This is Emily speaking. How may I help you?"

"Hello, Emily, my name is Anthony Porter, and I'm responding to your e-mail about the agent position."

"Thank you for getting back to me, Anthony. I need you to come to the office and finish the interview process. Could you be here within the next two hours?"

"Sure. What's the location?"

After Emily gave me the location, I got on the bus and pulled into Center City.

Once I got to the front desk, I checked in and waited for Emily to show up.

Twenty minutes later, a caramel-skinned woman in a navy blue business suit took purposeful strides toward me and had a stone expression on her face.

Her hair was pulled back into a basic ponytail, and she shook my hand with authority. She was all business.

"I have one simple rule, Anthony. Don't waste my time and I won't waste yours. Understand?"

"Yes, ma'am."

"This job is stressful. You're not guaranteed to get a bonus every month, and most people quit within the first few weeks. You tell me now if you can handle this position, or I can find someone else."

I took a deep breath. "I embrace new challenges, and I'm not a quitter. I'm ready for whatever."

"Good to hear," she said and led me on a tour throughout the building.

All in all, I spent an hour at the collection agency. Emily formally interviewed me, and I met a couple of the agents to get a feel of what my job duties would be.

"If we want to move forward, you will hear from us in about a month or so. If not, we've moved on to other candidates," she said without emotion.

I thanked her for the time and shook her hand.

Although I didn't admit it, I was a little pessimistic about taking the job. I felt like a hypocrite because I would be asking people for money they might've not had. I had been on the other side of the fence, and I sympathized with them and their situations. To put it bluntly, I hated collection agencies' harassment of people in financial trouble. Luckily for me, I hated being broke even more, so I pushed my personal feelings aside and prepared myself to be a debt collector.

It looked like Phaedra's would be in my rearview soon.

I felt confident that I would get the job.

March

So far, Quick Care proved to be a cool place to work at. The work wasn't difficult, and there was plenty of eye candy to keep me busy. Also knowing I had another potential job in the pipeline made my days more relaxing.

Sitting at work, all I could think about was my coworker Cassie. She had tennis ball-sized breasts and a perfectly rounded ass. Basically, she had a body specifically made to fill out bikinis and boy shorts. She wore her hair in a natural Afro, and she came off shy. We went to lunch a few times, and I enjoyed our time together. She thought I was handsome, and I would be lying if I said it wasn't flattering. If I was single, I would've definitely asked for her number.

After going out to lunch with her again, I went into the break room to get a book out of my locker. When I smelled Cassie's perfume, I froze in place.

"Hey, Anthony," she whispered in my ear and let her lips graze my earlobe.

I swallowed hard and said, "Hey."

She reached around and touched my crotch, and I became excited. When I spun around, I noticed her nipples were straining against her work shirt. The temptation was too much. I pulled her close and buried my face in her cleavage, and she moaned. She gently grabbed my face and kissed me. Her lips were as soft as rose petals. Soon our tongues touched, and I squeezed her ass with both hands. Then I pulled away.

"I'm sorry," I said and wiped the lip gloss from my lips.

"Don't be." She tried to touch me again.

I spared her one last glance before I stormed out of the break room.

For the rest of my shift, I ignored her.

After I got off work, I stopped at the liquor store for vodka before I went home. Later on that night, I waited for Essence to fall asleep before I made a cup of coffee with vodka in it.

I felt like shit because, in a moment of weakness, I contemplated cheating on Essence. Cassie and I clicked, and I thought she was attractive. I shouldn't have kissed her, but it felt so damn good. I promised myself I would right the ship.

Our lunches were dead, and I had to keep my distance. I didn't want this to be a bigger deal than it had to be.

Once I finished my drink, I drifted off to sleep thinking that I dodged a bullet by not going further with Cassie then I could've.

The next morning, I slipped out from underneath the covers and got a jump start on the day planning. Thinking Essence needed some pampering, I called up the salon she went to and set up a pedicure, manicure, and hair appointment for her. I needed to get my mind off of Cassie, and spending time with Essence would do the trick.

After I showered and got dressed in a T-shirt and sweats, I went downstairs and cooked breakfast. I made us blueberry pancakes, brown sugar bacon, and cheesy over easy eggs with fresh fruit. I took the food upstairs to the bedroom.

Once I got to her side of the bed, she looked up at me and yawned.

"About time you woke up," I said and smiled.

"Good morning to you too." Her face lit up when she saw the food. "Is that for me?"

"Sure is." I handed her the plate. "You eat up and get dressed. There are more surprises to come." I kissed her on the forehead and made my way back down to the kitchen.

I put Tupperware containers full of food and snacks and a bottle of wine in a travel tote bag. A picnic seemed like something cool to try.

I put the bag in the car and went back in the house to watch basketball highlights on ESPN.

An hour and a half passed before Essence came down the stairs. The time wasn't wasted either. She wore a royal blue sundress that showed off her butt and breasts. The flats she wore showed off her pretty feet.

"Okay, so where are we going?" She grabbed her keys and purse off the coffee table.

"It's a surprise."

"I think I like the sound of that."

"I figured you would." I rubbed my hands together.

After Essence finished up at the salon, we went to the Philadelphia Museum of Art. We saw beautiful artwork by some talented artists. The sculptures and portraits were unbelievable.

We held hands as we walked around talking, laughing, and looking at the exhibits. We didn't know a lot about art, but some of the pictures held our attention better than others.

"This is a lot better than us fighting." Essence smiled.

"Yes, it is," I said and kissed her on the cheek.

An hour after we left the museum, we went to Rittenhouse Square. Sunshine peeked through the clouds, and the breeze was perfect. The day couldn't have been any better.

I laid a blanket down on the grass under a tree. Inside the bag, I had assorted cheeses, grapes, chocolates, turkey, Asiago sandwiches, and Sangria.

"Today has been perfect, Anthony," Essence said when she saw the spread.

"It's all for you." I kissed the back of her hand.

She leaned over and kissed me on the cheek.

We fed each other food and sipped wine. Then, I French-kissed her. Knowing where this could head, she stopped me. Somehow, she had the same glow as when we first met each other.

"You ever think about us growing old together?" Essence asked.

I stroked her hair and touched her cheek. "Yes. I've been thinking of us a lot. Where we are and where we're headed."

She put her hands on top of mine. "Me too."

We kissed, again, this one longer than the last.

Pulling Essence close to me, I inhaled her perfume and nuzzled her neck. These were the moments that were priceless to me.

"I think we should meet each other's parents," I said.

"I was going to suggest the same thing to you. For our relationship to go to the next level, I think it's something we need to do."

"I agree."

"If we do this, you know what's next, right?"

"What's that?"

"Marriage and babies," she said and smiled.

She did pique my curiosity. Visions of her flowing ivory-colored wedding dress and us on our honeymoon on a tropical island flashed in my mind. Then I saw kids that looked like Essence and me combined.

Then I saw debt and added responsibility. Reality hit me hard in that instant.

"That's a lot of responsibility. I just don't think we're quite there yet."

All the color drained from her face, and she tilted her head when she looked at me. "*Really? Are we going to play house forever, or are we going to make our relationship real?*"

"So you're implying it isn't real now?" I asked. I was curious now. She opened a can of worms.

"I'm saying I'm not trying to play house with you forever."

"When it's the right time for marriage and kids, trust me, we'll know. Have some patience."

She rolled her eyes and sucked her teeth. "I hope it doesn't take as long as you did to find another job."

"You just couldn't go one day without starting some shit with me? You really like drama, and it's sickening," I said, my arms flailing.

"You're entitled to your opinion. I'm just telling you how I feel." She folded her arms across her chest.

"Why do you like pissing me off?"

She ignored my question and stood. "Patience to you obviously means forever."

I stood too. "I don't jump into things blindly."

"Only when it's important to you."

I blew out a frustrated breath and then smiled. "Thank you for fucking the day up."

"I'm ready to go," Essence said and started walking back to the Benz.

"Good, because so am I." I packed up everything and followed behind her.

As soon as I got in the car, Essence got on her cell phone. She was on one of her childish fits. Just when things were going in the right direction, here she comes with some more bullshit.

She went from zero to sixty so quick it was scary. Despite her pissing me off, she still looked so beautiful. It made me think of the lyrics to a song by Jimmy Cozier called "She's All I Got."

"Sometimes I love her. Sometimes I love her not. I ain't letting her go 'cause she's all I got. Although she nags me and complains a lot, I ain't letting her go. No, no, no."

April

I was excited to meet Essence's parents. I wasn't sure her meeting my mother would go over too well. Although my mother was supportive of me, I'm certain her support had its limits.

From what Essence told me, her parents seemed okay. Then again, she wouldn't paint them to be anything but upstanding and good people. I knew what fathers thought of their daughters, and I was a little shook about what her stepfather thought of me. If I got his approval, I had an advantage. If I didn't get his approval, I was in deep trouble.

Another thing Essence told me was that her stepfather was judgmental and that it would be a good idea if I wore dress clothes.

That's why I sat on the edge of our bed tying my dress shoes. I even shaved my face clean.

You only get one first impression, and I didn't want to blow it. Keeping things simple, I wore black slacks and a white dress shirt.

As I stood in the mirror, Essence came up behind me and smiled.

"You look perfect."

"Thank you," I said and kissed her on the cheek.

She adjusted my collar. "Now let's get out of here. We don't want to be late."

I admired her hip-hugging dress and smiled. "No, we don't."

As we navigated our way through Center City traffic, I thought about how things became tense at Quick Care. For a few days, Cassie gave me the silent treatment. Not being able to stand it any longer, I sent her a message through our work e-mail.

She agreed to meet me for lunch. I told her I had a girl, and that while I thought she was attractive, I wouldn't step out on Essence. She said she respected my honesty, and we agreed to be cordial to each other. It gave me one less thing to stress over. So far, so good.

I became so stuck in my thoughts that I didn't notice Essence parallel parking.

"You ready?" she asked.

"Of course. I can't wait to meet your folks," I said genuinely happy to meet them.

Letting the thoughts of Cassie dissolve, I stepped out of the car and zipped my jacket up. The downtown sidewalks were littered with people going every which way.

Essence hit a button to lock the door, and we were on our way. I had no idea where the heck we were going, and Essence wasn't trying to give me any hints either.

Two blocks later, we rounded the corner and entered the lobby of a steakhouse called Del Frisco's. Just by the people that populated the place, I could tell this spot was a big deal. I was sure I saw a few professional athletes and business types in there with us. Essence nudged me when a couple approached us in the lobby.

Here was the moment of truth.

"Hey, Daddy!" Essence squealed and jumped into her stepfather's muscular arms.

"Hey, baby girl."

Then she hugged her mother.

Her stepfather scared the shit out of me. He sported a curly 'fro, a neat beard, and had a football player's build. His square jaw seemed to be made of steel, and his stare was cold.

Essence's mother had golden skin, warm eyes, and a genuine smile. I hoped Essence aged that well. Neither of her parents looked a day over thirty-five.

"You must be Anthony." Essence's stepfather and I shook hands. "I'm Robert, and this is my wife, Tina."

"Nice to meet you both, sir."

"How come we are just meeting Anthony?" Essence's stepfather asked her.

"I told you, Daddy. I wasn't sure how serious we were going to be. That's all in the past. Let's focus on the here and now."

"Okay. Whatever you say, baby girl," he said and dropped the issue as we all walked in the dimly lit restaurant.

The high ceilings, polished floors, and wood finishing screamed luxury.

We were seated within ten minutes despite the people in front of us. I didn't miss the fact that Essence's stepfather whispered in the maître d's ear either.

They sat us at a table in the center of the restaurant.

It seemed like the staff went to extra lengths to please Essence's stepfather.

"What kind of pull does your stepfather have in here?" I whispered in her ear.

"He's golfing buddies with the manager."

I shook my head and smiled. "That's explains a lot."

After the waiter took our drink orders, Essence's stepfather went right in on me. "How old are you, Anthony?"

"I'm nineteen, sir."

His eyebrows shot up in surprise, and he leaned back in his chair.

"Wow, Essence. You didn't tell me Anthony was a teenager." He looked over at her.

"I didn't think it was a big deal," she said nonchalantly.

"Now you know your mother was a cougar too." He gave his wife a knowing smile. Then he looked back at me. "I like my woman older too, Anthony. Nothing wrong with that, son."

After we shared a laugh, Mr. Dwyer became serious again.

"Are you employed?"

"Yes, sir."

"Good . . . good." He put his napkin in his lap. "Where do you see yourself in five years?"

Clearing my throat, I said, "I hope to enjoy a successful career and be married with children." I left out everything about screenwriting on purpose. I wouldn't let him judge me on my dreams.

"I'm surprised you don't want to be a rapper, basketball player, or stand on the street corner and peddle drugs." His glare was ice cold, but I wouldn't be broken no matter what he tried.

"No disrespect, sir, but you shouldn't be surprised. I got a good head on my shoulders." I didn't break eye contact with him.

"So you're telling me you don't have any illegitimate kids, drinking habits, or drug problems I should know about?"

"No, sir. I'm not a hoodlum, and I don't appreciate being questioned like one."

"I don't mean to be rude, but the wool has been pulled over my eyes before," he said and shot daggers at Essence.

"I understand, sir. Just know I'm nothing like them."

"Daddy, please, let the past be in the past," Essence pleaded.

"Give the boy a chance, Robert," Mrs. Dwyer said and slapped her husband on the shoulder.

Essence put her hand on mine to let me know she supported me, and I appreciated the gesture.

When I looked at the menu prices I almost flipped out. I assumed that this place was expensive, but they were trying to kill me. Now I wish we would've gone to Chili's or Applebee's. Basically, something affordable.

The waiter came back with our drinks and took our food orders. When he got to Essence, she ordered the sixty-nine dollar bone-in filet, and I had the filet mignon to keep up appearances.

Although I was steaming on the inside, I played it cool on the outside. I couldn't look cheap in front of her father.

After we ate dinner, I felt like Essence's parents and I got to know one another better. In some ways, I felt closer to Essence through her people. Learning that she was a tomboy made me laugh. Her father was a pediatrician, and her mother was a housewife. She was used to being taken care of. At least I knew where Essence got it from.

"I'm glad I finally got to meet you guys today," I said.

"The feeling's mutual, son." Essence's stepfather gave her the side eye.

I laughed when he did that. My smile faded when the waiter came to the table with the bill. Essence went for her purse, and I grabbed her arm. I felt like her parents were watching me. I had to show and prove.

"Don't embarrass me," I whispered to her.

I became salty when I noticed we spent over $200 on dinner. After I paid our portion of the tab and took a deep breath, I reasoned that the experience was worth the trouble. If I would be accepted into the fold, I didn't care about the money.

We said our good-byes and walked outside. Before Essence and I got around the corner, her stepfather stopped me. Essence gave us some space to talk.

"I'm glad my daughter found you, son. And I'm not one to bad-mouth people, but you're an improvement over the men she's been with over the years." He pulled me into a fatherly hug. "You two make a great couple, and I'm happy to have you in the family."

"Thank you, sir."

"Oh, and one more thing."

"Yes, sir."

"Dinner was on me. I got the manager to refund you the cost of your meal. That will be our little secret."

I smiled, and we shook hands before he and Mrs. Dwyer got into a champagne-colored BMW.

Essence looped her arm into mine. "That wasn't so bad now, was it?"

"Of course not. Your folks are good people. I'm glad I met them."

"So am I."

Essence and I got into the car.

"I can tell your stepfather really cares about you and your mother."

"He's always been a bright spot in my life," she said and smiled.

I smiled too. "I'm glad you have him."

"Me too." She started the car. "Now it's time to meet your mother."

"You sure you ready?"

"Are you sure?"

Only time would tell.

April

I put a pot of coffee on and went through the mail. Four out of the ten envelopes I opened were credit card and payday loan offers. I ripped open the fifth envelope. The screenwriting contest people were cc'd in the letter. I read the letter out loud.

Dear Sir or Ma'am,

Thank you for your screenplay submission. Unfortunately, this work does not fit the needs of the studio at this time. We wish you well in your future endeavors.

I closed my eyes and rubbed my temples after I opened and read the contents of the remaining envelopes. Not only did the screenwriting contest people turn me down, but the film agencies in Los Angeles sent me, *"your project doesn't fit our needs at this time"* stock letters.

Pissed off by the news, I burst into the kitchen and got vodka from my hiding place. Unexpectedly, Essence came into the kitchen and scared the hell out of me. I almost dropped the bottle on the floor.

"Everything okay?" I asked, more out of nervousness than anything else.

"I forgot the car charger." She saw the vodka bottle in my hand. "Why are you drinking alcohol so early in the morning?" She looked at me like I sprouted another head.

Feeling embarrassed, I didn't say anything. I had always been supercareful not to drink around her, and now I had let the cat out of the bag.

"It's 9:30 in the damn morning, Anthony. You have some serious issues if you're getting loaded this early."

"I needed something stronger than coffee. Get off my back about it. I'm really not in the mood to be judged by you right now."

"Real funny, Anthony. How long has this drinking in the morning thing been going on for?"

Her tone became super judgmental and accusatory.

"What does it matter anyway?"

"If you're drinking this early, there's something you're not telling me."

"There's nothing to tell." I poured vodka into a cup of coffee and took a sip.

"I'm legally able to drink. You aren't. Big difference." Her voice was stern. "Are you starting to get the picture now?"

"*Casual* drinking hasn't been a problem for me, and it never will be." I pointed the coffee cup at her. "We've drunk together plenty of times before. So get off of your soapbox."

"I won't support an alcoholic."

I put the cup down and got in her face. "Where do you get off calling me an alcoholic? You're jumping to conclusions."

"I'm just calling it like I see it."

"Maybe you're seeing it wrong."

"You really need some help."

"Fuck you," I said, seething.

She went over and grabbed the wall charger and smiled at me before she went toward the door. "I won't be disrespected by you. You wanna be an asshole, you can find your own place to live."

Between Emily Waters not getting back to me and the sting of rejection, I was on level ten of being frustrated. Getting loaded seemed like the only sensible thing to do at the time. So I poured the rest of the vodka in my coffee cup and had a pity party.

Since it was my day off, I took a nap, and when I woke up, I had a voice mail from my mother. I called her cell phone.

"Hey, son. How are you?" my mother asked.

"I just woke up. Is everything okay?" I yawned.

"Of course. I miss you. I miss hearing your voice."

That made me smile. "I miss you too, Mom."

"Anything new and exciting happening?"

"I met Essence's parents."

"I suppose you want me to meet her, right?"

"Maybe . . . Well . . . If it's not a problem with you." I crossed my fingers.

"Give me some time to think about it."

"I guess that's better than no."

She sighed. "I still want what's best for you and . . ." she trailed off.

"And she's not what's best for me?"

"I think you can do better. You have to be patient, and I believe the right woman will come along."

"Once you get to know Essence, I think you'll have a different opinion of her."

"Maybe," she said unenthusiastically.

"I'm just asking you to give her a shot."

"My break is almost over, and I have to get back to work, baby."

I sighed. "I love you, Mom."

"I love you too."

She disconnected the call.

The Yahoo! e-mail notification popped up on my phone. I opened the e-mail and Emily Waters sent me an offer letter detailing my health benefits, work schedule, and starting salary.

The position had great benefits, and the pay was phenomenal. I almost did a backflip when I got done reading through all the documents.

Then I got to her message at the bottom of the e-mail:

I apologize for the inconvenience, but the start date has to be pushed back to July.

April

The next time I went into work, Phaedra called me into her office. She had on a low cut top and a push-up bra. I tried not to stare at her breasts, but it was hard not to.

"I appreciate you being professional about the changes around here, and I have some good news . . . I can give you three shifts instead of just one."

"Seriously?" I asked skeptically. I had been in her office too many times about this same thing. I was just about numb at this point.

"I can guarantee you those additional days during the week," she said and offered a warm and disarming smile.

It was too late. I had my mind set on getting out of this job and moving on to greener pastures. They had played around too many times with my hours. I didn't want to be flapping in the wind when the next inevitability happened. I would take the hours and make my move in July.

"Thank you so much for looking out for me, Phaedra. I really appreciate it," I said smiling.

"It's no problem. You're a hard worker, and if I can help in any way, I will. Hopefully, there will be more good news to come."

"I hope so, and thank you again."

When I got back home after work, Essence was at the stove cooking dinner. I hugged her from behind. I messed up and said some things I didn't mean, and I needed to get back on her good side.

"You're wasting your time by touching me," she said and didn't turn around.

Ignoring her attitude, I rubbed on her breasts and nipples. She swatted me away. I tried to touch her breasts again, and she faced me.

"Look, Anth—" she started to say.

Before she could push me away, I sucked on her neck and squeezed on her ass.

She hit me in the shoulder weakly. "No, Anthony. Stop."

I pinned her arms against the wall and kissed her shoulder blade, neck, cheek, and lips. With her eyes closed, she bit her lip. She was putty in my hands. She moaned as I pulled her panties to the side and rubbed on her throbbing clit.

"Let me get a condom," I said.

I went to go upstairs, and she grabbed my wrist. "No," she said. "Not tonight."

We went over to the couch. She took her panties all the way off and spread her legs open for me. Loving her sweet smell, I buried my face in her crotch. She smelled like Fruity Pebbles.

We tried to outdo each other sexually. We must have switched positions three or four times. Neither one of us wanted to give in.

Once she came, I followed right behind her. Then we snuggled.

"I shouldn't have cursed at you when you caught me drinking. Sometimes I don't know how to express myself, and it comes out wrong. I'm sorry for that," I said.

"I'm sorry too. I shouldn't have called you an alcoholic. You were having a bad day, and I should've respected that."

"I had got a bunch of rejection letters, and I needed a drink to numb the pain."

"You just remember that it's their loss. When you make it to the top, you can look back and laugh at the idiots who didn't believe in you."

"So you believe in me, huh?"

"A hundred percent, baby."

"I appreciate that."

"Always."

"And I promise the drinking is not an issue."

"Okay," she said and touched my hand.

I took a deep breath and changed the subject. "You think your parents liked me?"

"I'm certain they did."

"How can you be so sure?" I'm all for positivity, but they could've expressed something different to Essence behind the scenes. You never know.

"They're pretty straightforward. They would've told you to your face if they didn't like you."

"I'm glad they liked me then."

"Me too."

"I can't wait for you to meet my mother."

"I'm looking forward to it."

"You know they say your wife is a reflection of your mother."

"Then your mother must be pretty special."

"She's one of a kind," I said, smiling.

I pulled Essence closer to me and nuzzled her neck.

When I went to sleep that night, I prayed hard that my mother would accept Essence with open arms.

Prayer was all I had.

May

The butterflies in my stomach wouldn't stop fluttering. Basically, I played with fire by having Essence and my mother meet each other. I had to do something because if I wanted a future with Essence, I needed her and my mother to be on the same page.

I sat at my mother's dining-room table holding Michael, who had drifted off to sleep. My mother stood at the stove stirring spaghetti sauce. The kitchen smelled like garlic.

"You're allowed to visit us more than just once in a while," she said over her shoulder.

"I know, and I promise you I'll visit more when I get some downtime. I been working a little more than usual." She was right, but I needed some type of excuse to tell her. I needed to visit her more, and I planned to.

"You'd better. No matter what, you're still my baby. We may butt heads and disagree on things, but that doesn't mean I don't love you or want to see you."

"I love you too," I said and smiled. I looked at my cell phone and shook my head. Essence was late. She had pissed me off because she knew how important this was to me.

"I'll be right back, Mom. I'm going to put him to bed." I took Michael upstairs to the bedroom and then went outside.

Essence and I agreed she would be there at seven-thirty so we could eat dinner with my mother. While I paced the sidewalk, I mumbled to myself. I called Essence on her cell phone and got her voice mail. Where the hell was she at?

A few minutes later, I looked back across the street as she parked behind my mother's neighbor's car.

"Hey, baby," she said after she got out of the car and came over to me.

"You're late." I pointed to my wrist, scowling.

"I'm so sorry. I got caught up in traffic. I should've left the job earlier to make it here on time. You ready?"

"Of course. I was born ready," I said with a smile.

"Let's make it happen then."

We walked hand in hand up the steps and into the house. Every step I took, it felt like bricks were strapped to my ankles.

When we got into the kitchen, I braced myself. "Anthony, I need—" my mother said as she turned around. "You didn't tell me we had a guest." She looked Essence up and down. "I'm Anthony's mother, Brenda, but you can call me Ms. Porter."

They shook hands unenthusiastically.

Essence put on a phony smile and nodded. "Nice to meet you, Ms. Porter."

I grabbed three plates out of the cabinet and put them on the table. After I made all of our plates and poured us lemonade, we sat down at the table to eat.

The tension in the room was thick.

I tried to break the ice. "I'm glad we all got a chance to enjoy a meal together."

Essence and my mother sighed right after each other.

"Can we all talk like civilized people?" I asked, not liking where this was headed.

"Tell me something," my mother began, crossing her arms and addressing Essence, "what does a twenty-nine-year-old woman want with a teenager?" She went right in. She didn't have a chill button.

"Mom, can you relax?" I asked, my arms flailing.

"It's cool, Anthony," Essence said and sipped her lemonade. She directed her attention back to my mother. "Age ain't nothing but a number. I love your son, and he loves me. Nothing you do or say will change that," she said with much attitude.

"What's the problem? Nobody your age wants your ass?" my mother asked and smiled sarcastically.

Essence shook her head. "I'm a grown-ass woman just like you are, so please miss me with the disrespect."

"You may have Anthony fooled, but I know you're a predator."

Essence smiled. "You're entitled to your opinion."

"I know I am cradle robber." I gave my mother the death stare, and she just shrugged.

Essence ignored my mother and said, "Anthony, can you pass me the salt and pepper, please."

Nobody said anything while we ate. The only thing that could be heard was our forks scraping our plates.

Once we finished with dinner, Essence told me, "I'll be in the car." Before she got up from the table, she kissed me on the mouth just to annoy my mother.

"I'll be out there soon." When Essence left, I directed my attention to my mother. "Really, Mom? You *had* to go there, didn't you?"

She looked up at me indifferently. "All I'm doing is calling it like I see it. You can't see what I see, and I don't blame you. I'm not the one in love. You are."

"You didn't even give her a chance," I said with a scowl.

"Maybe she isn't worth the chance."

I looked at my mother in disbelief. I always thought there was a glimmer of hope in regards to Essence and my mother's relationship. Obviously, I was dead wrong.

"This isn't about you. This is about me finding someone that I love, and who loves me back. If you can't be happy for me, then you can kiss my ass." My voice cracked with emotion.

I stormed outside and hopped in the car. I punched the dashboard so hard my hand hurt.

Essence touched my hand. "I'm sorry, Anthony. I wish this didn't happen."

"She didn't have to do that."

"You don't need her approval for us to be together."

"I know, but I wanted her support. That's the least she could do."

"You have to accept that she might never warm up to our relationship."

My heart hurt because Essence was right. My mother might never be happy for me and our relationship. She played me, and for the time being, I didn't have shit else to say to her.

June

Essence and my mother meeting each other sounded like a good idea on paper. Stupidly, I thought something positive would come of their meeting. Essence and I hadn't talked about the incident since it happened, and I didn't plan on bringing it up either. There wasn't much more to say.

Sometimes I think positivity killed Essence. Whenever things were going too right, she had a tendency to incorporate negativity into our lives. This day was no different.

As I sat at the dining-room table using the laptop, Essence interrupted my flow with one of her bitching sessions.

"We need to be at my parents' house by two o'clock. Can you get off the Internet for one minute?" She walked up the stairs and stopped. "And another thing. You need to get a driver's license. I'm tired of being your damn chauffeur."

I pushed back from the table and got up. "Let's be real with each other, Essence. This isn't about me being on the Internet or me needing to drive. What's this really about? Be honest with yourself."

She came all the way back down the stairs and stood at the bottom. She folded her arms across her chest, and her eyes narrowed to slits.

"This is about everything I've let fly around here. I'm sick of babying you."

"And how exactly do you baby me?"

"Let me count the ways. You don't drive, and you haven't shown yourself to be proactive at all since we've been together. Anything to do with household concerns gets pushed to the backburner."

"Where is all this coming from?"

"I'm just tired of being silent about things around here."

I rubbed my face and sighed. "You want me to get my driver's license? Cool, I'll get one. Don't just complain about shit. Help me move forward."

"Help you? I've been carrying you the whole time we've been together."

"Wow. So now I'm a charity case?"

"If the shoe fits," she shrugged.

"How about you go to your parents' house alone. How's that?" I smiled sarcastically.

"I told them we'd be there at a certain time. Don't make me look stupid."

"Everything is about looks with you. Because I don't have a license, that looks bad. Because I don't make as much money as you, that looks bad. Get a grip on reality."

"No. That's where you're wrong. This is about you being irresponsible. This is about me having to bitch and moan for things to get done around here. I'd be shocked if you did anything on your own without me telling you to."

"You talk about wanting to be married and have children, and you behave like this? It's okay to chill out sometimes."

"That's your problem. You're too lackadaisical. If it's not important to Anthony, then it doesn't get your full attention."

"You know what, Essence? You win. I'm a terrible person who doesn't make you happy. There, I said it. Satisfied? I'll be outside in the car," I said and stormed off.

For the first time in our relationship, Essence was speechless. I went outside and left her standing there stuck on stupid.

A few minutes later, we were in the car driving to her parents' house. The entire time I talked on the phone just to piss her off. Anything she threw at me I planned to throw back at her.

Petty would be my middle name.

June

For the next week, I took a practice driving test on the Internet until I got a passing score. I was tired of Essence's bitching and complaining. More importantly, I hated not being self-sufficient. Essence's message couldn't have been clearer, but her delivery was off. I wanted to be free of her grip. If I could stand alone, our relationship would be better off in the long run.

I called in sick for work on a Wednesday morning and went to the DMV, where I sat in the waiting area for an hour before they called me in to take the driving test.

My palms rained sweat, and I tapped my foot as I sat there in front of the bright computer monitor. Methodically, I took my time with every question and eventually walked out of the DMV with my driver's license. My heart swelled with pride knowing I would legally be able to get behind the wheel.

After I got off the bus from downtown, I came home and found Essence sitting at the dining-room table. I sat next to her.

"I got some good news," I said and smiled proudly.

Essence rolled her eyes. "What is it?"

I slapped my driver's license down on the table as a response.

Her eyes lit up like Times Square, and she jumped out of her seat to come and kiss me.

"I'm so proud of you. All I want you to do is be self-sufficient. My delivery sucked, but I had good intentions." She sat back down.

"Your delivery did suck, but your message was very clear."

"Sometimes I get so riled up, and by the time I realize the harshness of my words, it's too late."

I touched her hand. "We aren't perfect, and I understand that. In the future, I would like for you to tell me what you want without confrontation."

"I can do that."

"You sure?"

"I promise."

"I'm holding you to that."

"I know."

"Now I just gotta get a car of my own."

She smiled devilishly. "In the meantime, you wanna test drive the Benz?"

"Hell, yeah."

She put the car keys in my hand and went up the stairs.

"You're not coming?" I asked, shocked.

She stopped on the staircase. "No, I'm not. You're a big boy. You can handle it."

Then she disappeared upstairs.

I revved the engine for a few seconds before I pulled out of the parking spot. Driving around the city, taking in the sights and sounds felt empowering. It also made me realize how much I needed to have my own vehicle. Something that I could put in my name.

When I got back home that night I called my mother. I needed to mend fences.

"Hello, Mister Kiss-ass. How are you?"

"Mom, I—"

She cut me off.

"You got some nerve calling here."

"I called to say I'm sorry."

"I didn't raise you to be disrespectful, and I'm hurt and disappointed you would speak to me like that."

I felt ashamed because I let my emotions get the best of me, and I shouldn't have.

"I was wrong for what I said, but I stand by why I said it, though."

She laughed. "I see this girl got your nose wide open, huh?"

"She does. You may not like my relationship, but I do ask that you respect it."

"Respect is earned."

"I know. That's why I'm calling you like a man to say I was out of line, and it won't happen again."

"Oh, I know it won't happen again. If it does happen again, I'm going to bust your ass."

I smiled. "I love you, Mom."

"I love you too, son."

I was back on speaking terms with my mother and I had my driver's license. Now if I found me an agent, I would be batting a thousand.

July

I hit a brick wall like Wile E. Coyote in regards to gaining any traction with finding an agent or shining a spotlight on my screenplays.

I really felt like going through Kickstarter would be the last resort. If I wasn't able to secure an agent, I would turn to the crowdfunding platform. Through extensive research, I found out the system was pretty simple. There were a lot of articles on how to launch a successful Kickstarter campaign. I went with the ones that made the most sense to me.

One of the articles I read said to set a realistic goal, so I set the goal at $6,000. When I tallied what I needed to make a short film, the amount would be more than enough.

The program would run thirty days, and I planned on passing out business cards for people to pledge funds. My Web site would be on the card, and what they would get out of pledging would be on the front page.

I had my business plan written, and I was ready to roll. I felt it in my bones that it was my destiny to be a part of Hollywood.

In addition to starting the Kickstarter program, I also wrote a resignation letter. I appreciated Phaedra for giving me an opportunity, but I needed to move on, and I had my mind made up already. I needed peace of mind more than anything.

Just as Essence came into the door from work, I waved her over to the dining-room table. I sipped cold coffee.

"You okay?" she asked.

"I'm nervous about this thing that I started."

"What is it?"

"You ever heard of a program called Kickstarter?"

"No."

"Me either, until I did some research. Basically, people donate money toward the completion of your independent project."

"And strangers just blindly give you money?" She went to the kitchen and poured herself a cup of coffee and came back to the table.

"I thought it was crazy too, but some people just like to support a good cause."

"No offense, baby, but what do they get out of it?"

"I would put their name in the credits and give them a T-shirt and a gift card. It's not much, but it's something."

"Don't sell yourself short. That's a fair enough exchange in my opinion."

"You really think so?"

"Of course."

I smiled and went to get another cup of coffee and put ice cubes in it.

"If this is going to work, I'm going to need your help."

"Sure. Anything you need."

"If you could hand out some business cards at your job, I would really appreciate it."

"No problem at all."

"I'm lucky to have you," I stood and kissed her on the lips.

She smiled. "The feeling is mutual."

After Essence and I watched TV and she dozed off, I sent a quick text message to my mother and Paul asking for their help with the Kickstarter campaign.

Eventually, I fell asleep thinking about how happy I would be if I hit my Kickstarter goal.

July

I'm not a morning person, but I got up bright and early so I could turn in my resignation letter to Phaedra. It was Paul's birthday that day too, and I had a surprise lined up for him. Before I left the house, I drank a spiked cup of coffee just to loosen me up. Then I grabbed my wallet and house keys and bounced.

My normal commute took longer because of miscellaneous road work. Despite that, I couldn't stop smiling. Just thinking about this new opportunity at the collection agency got me hyped.

I walked through Phaedra's feeling like a fish in a fishbowl. For some reason, all eyes were on me. I shrugged it off. When Phaedra saw me, she waved me into her office. Something felt off about her, and I couldn't put my finger on it.

"Close the door," Phaedra said, her eyes looking tired. "I appreciated the work you did here. You were a great employee, and . . ." she began.

"Are you firing me?" I cut her off.

"It looks like we jumped the gun a little bit. We need to trim the fat, and you got caught in the crossfire. I'm truly sorry about this." The sadness in her eyes was genuine.

For a split second I felt hollow. The news was like an uppercut to the chin. Then I quickly realized I had another job lined up, and I still had my part-time gig.

My frown melted into a smile, and I hugged Phaedra and thanked her for the opportunity.

She seemed shocked that I was taking this all in stride. Before I left the restaurant, I said good-bye to my coworkers.

Then I took the bus to Mitchell & Ness. I showed the salesperson a cell phone picture of the warm-up jacket I wanted, and he rang me up. I wore the Vancouver Grizzlies warm-up jacket out of the store.

Since I was downtown already, I went to Foot Locker in the Gallery Mall and bought some new sneakers.

Once I left the store, I sent Paul a text message:

You got any birthday plans?

Not really. I was trying to see what you were up to.

If you down, I got an idea.

I'm down. What's up?

Paul agreed to meet me at Barnes & Noble after he got off work, and I made sure I had cash on me. I needed to tell Essence about losing my job, but that could wait. I just wanted my boy to enjoy his birthday.

Around 6:30 p.m. that night, Paul picked me up outside the bookstore.

"You feeling good?" I asked.

"Absolutely, bro. How about you?"

"I was until I got to work today."

"What happened?"

"I got fired from Phaedra's."

"Are you serious?"

"Unfortunately."

"You still got the other gig lined up, right?"

"I do."

"You good then, bro."

"I'm hoping so."

"Don't worry about that situation. Once you get this new job, Phaedra's will be a distant memory."

"Amen to that."

Paul stopped at a stop sign. "So where are we going, bro?"

"Good question."

"So, basically, you're not going to tell me."

"Nope, but I'll give you directions."

Paul drove along Columbus Boulevard, and then we turned into a crowded parking lot. He circled the parking lot for ten minutes until someone pulled out and he took their spot.

Once Paul saw the sign with a blue illuminated silhouette of a woman, he knew we were at a strip club. I found out about the place on the Internet. Paul couldn't scramble out of the truck fast enough. I had never been to a gentleman's club before, and I was excited to see some naked women too.

I paid our cover charges at the door, and I got hit in the chest with heavy bass from the loud hip-hop music blaring through the speakers.

"Thanks for bringing me here," Paul said as we ventured deeper into the dimly lit club. The air smelled like sweet perfume, sweat, and Buffalo wings.

"I remember you said we need to hit up a strip club. There's no time like the present," I said. I rubbed my hands together as a pink thong-wearing big booty stripper pranced by.

We found a small table in the back corner of the club and ordered some drinks.

I sipped Cîroc and lemonade and watched the thick woman on stage work the pole like she owned it. The club allowed full nudity, so when she slid down the pole with her legs open, she showcased all her business. I hungrily licked my lips as the claps and cheers rained down on the woman.

The music abruptly cut off, and there was silence for a few moments.

"What's going on?" Paul asked, confused.

I patted him on the shoulder. "My gift to you. Happy Birthday."

A spotlight shined on the spot the last stripper just vacated. Then the DJ said, "Put your hands together for Ms. Sapphire!"

The place exploded in whistles, claps, and cheers. Ciara's "Ride" played in the background as she gyrated with the beat.

She was our favorite porn star.

Her skin was the color of coffee beans, and her jet-black hair tickled her shoulders. I personally spent many nights searching her videos on the Internet. I salivated over her horse ass, chunky thighs, and double D cup breasts. We locked eyes while she moved her hips from side to side. By the time she finished her set, the floor was a mess of dollar bills. I threw about fifty dollars up there myself.

I gave Paul an animated handshake. "This is the best birthday gift ever, bro!" he yelled.

"That's what I wanted to hear!"

We ordered another round of Cîroc and lemonades. Feeling jittery, I waited for my chance to approach Sapphire, and once I got close enough, I felt a hand on my chest. I looked to her, and she gave the offensive lineman-built security guard the okay to let me pass.

I couldn't even look her in the eye because she was so beautiful. She smelled like peach-scented perfume, and I almost had a heart attack when she pulled me close and whispered into my ear, "Tell me what you want."

I closed my eyes and said, "Me and my boy want a lap dance. He can go first."

"Sure thing," she said and walked into the private room a few feet away from the main stage.

"Seventy-five," the well-built security guard said with a stone facial expression.

Without hesitation, I slapped the money into his palm and waved Paul over. I gave Paul a stack of one dollar bills on the sly and whispered in his ear. "Enjoy yourself."

"No doubt."

While Paul got acquainted with Sapphire, I watched the other girls dance on stage and threw a couple of singles. I came for the main attraction, and all the other girls felt insignificant at the moment.

Fifteen minutes later, Paul emerged from the darkened room, and Sapphire summoned me with a curled finger. I never moved that fast in my adult life. I almost knocked over a table, I was so anxious to get to her.

When I got into the darkened room, Sapphire guided me to the padded seat that wrapped around the small room. As the R&B music pumped through the small speakers in the room, she bounced her gigantic ass on my crotch. I became hard beneath her, and when she reached back and squeezed my package through my jeans, I almost lost it.

After the song switched, she straddled me and her breath smelled like spearmint. When she put her dime-sized nipples near my mouth, I sucked on them like a hungry infant. Then she kissed me on the neck, and I held on to her fluffy ass for dear life. Her soft kisses sent a jolt of energy throughout my body. Between the drinks I had and her perfume, I was on cloud nine.

I didn't want the lap dance to end, but when I heard banging on the door, I knew my dream had come to an end. Before Sapphire left the room, she kissed me on the cheek and disappeared back into the club.

I made my way back over to our table, and Paul had a huge smile on his face.

"How was it?" he asked excitedly.

"It felt like a dream. You know I watched every one of her videos, man."

"Me too, bro."

"How was it for you?"

"She let me do everything except stick it in."

"Really?"

"Yup."

"That's how you're supposed to enjoy your birthday!" I yelled, and we high-fived each other.

"Damn right, bro."

My cell phone vibrated in my pocket. It was a text from Essence:

Hope you guys are enjoying yourselves. I love you!

I sent back: We are, and I love you too

Then I noticed I had a voice mail and pressed the play button. It was Emily Waters from the collection agency.

"I'm sorry, Anthony, but your job offer has been rescinded."

July

When I got home after Paul and I left the strip club, I cried harder than I ever have. Every time I thought I did something right, it blew up in my face. To make matters worse, I found out I got offered the collections job because of a clerical error in human resources. I was supposed to get a rejection letter.

I took the weekend and the following Monday to cool off. Essence was super supportive and told me that I could lean on her. I needed to hear those words from her, and it helped to calm me down. I wasn't going to let this situation set me back. I was determined to get back out there and find an even better job. I was done with the stress and failure I kept feeling. The best thing I knew to do was to channel what I felt into finding another job.

I lumbered into work and needing a jolt of energy, I grabbed a cup of coffee from the break room. I planned on going to my boss to request some OT or even be moved up to full time. Anything to put more money in my pocket.

One of my busty coworkers came into the break room and seemed shocked to see me.

"I'm sorry about what happened . . ." she trailed off.

I was taken aback. "Sorry about what?" I said and finished my coffee, and then threw the plastic cup away.

"I shouldn't have said anything," she said and abruptly left the break room. When I went to follow her, my boss swung around the corner. Her eyes beamed with sadness. My shoulders slumped, and I went into panic mode. What the hell happened now?

"Anthony, I need you to come into my office," she said authoritatively.

I lumbered into her office and took a seat.

"Some troubling information has been relayed to me. I'm sure you know what I'm talking about."

"I'm not sure what you're talking about at all."

"Cassie said that you touched her inappropriately last week."

I pounded my fist on the table. "She's lying. I never touched her. I have a girl already."

"She said you grabbed her breasts." She looked at me skeptically.

I shook my head and laughed. This could not be happening to me. I had to be in the Twilight Zone.

"Like I said, I'm not guilty of anything. That girl is a flat-out liar." I folded my arms.

"We take these claims very seriously, and we're going to have to let you go. I'm sorry."

My eyes grew wide in disbelief. "Are you serious? This girl can just throw some bullshit claims out there, and y'all believe her? I've busted my ass at this job, and I can't get the benefit of the doubt?"

I was a lot of things, but I didn't touch women uninvited.

Here I thought Cassie and I had an understanding, but I was dead wrong.

"I wish there was something more I could do, but the decision isn't solely up to me. I have to play by the rules." She gave me a sympathetic look.

I felt like gum on the bottom of a dirty shoe. I lost two jobs in the same month and lost out on an opportunity for a third. Honestly, I didn't think I could sink any lower.

I flew out of my boss's office. Just the smell of the place made my stomach hurt. Looking at all the familiar faces when I walked out upset me. After I emptied out my locker, I kicked over a discarded mop bucket and smiled in delight when the dirty water covered the ground.

Before I went home, I bought a bottle of vodka from Wine and Spirits. I needed a stiff drink to take the edge off.

When I got home, I called Essence on her office line at work, and she answered in a cheery tone. By that time, I was on my second shot of vodka.

"Hey, you."

"Hey," I said flatly.

"You okay?"

"No. I got some more bad news."

"I'm listening."

"I got fired from Quick Care too."

"I'm so sorry, baby. Did they at least give you a good reason? Not that it means much."

"Not really," I lied.

"When I come home I can cook us some food and open a bottle of wine . . ."

"That sounds real nice right about now." I smiled because I definitely needed a distraction.

When I hung up the phone, I felt a little better.

Essence kept her word when she came home.

She made us shrimp Alfredo with garlic toast, and we had a little too much wine with dinner.

After we made passionate love I held her close to me as I stared at the ceiling. I felt like losing these two jobs was a sign. It was time to focus on my screenwriting 100 percent.

I had to show and prove.

August

Even with Paul's, my mother's, and Essence's support, I didn't meet my Kickstarter goal. The goal was $6,000, and the pledges only reached $2,500. I didn't meet the entire goal so no money changed hands.

Feeling bold and adventurous, I withdrew the last of my savings and hopped on a plane to Atlanta for a film conference down there.

It was seventy-seven degrees and sunny when I arrived at Hartsfield-Jackson Atlanta International Airport. I took an Uber to the Westin Hotel and settled in.

The city of Atlanta was beautiful, especially at night with all the bright lights and cool-looking skyline. The conference lasted four days, and a lot of heavy hitters in the film industry would be there. I took a shot of vodka to calm my nerves and went to bed.

The next morning, I wore business-casual clothing and had a few sips of spiked coffee before I went into my first pitch session. There were a lot of hopefuls sitting outside of the hotel conference room hoping their dream came true just like me. I sat there for a good forty minutes before a brown-skinned woman with a closely cropped haircut came and motioned for me to follow her.

The spiked coffee had me sweating. I wiped my face completely clean before I went into the conference room with the woman. I felt like the four people in the room were sharks, and they smelled blood in the water.

"Make it quick. We don't have all day," the woman who brought me in said.

I cleared my throat and pitched them my screenplay.

At the end of my pitch, they gave me a standing ovation. Their acceptance boosted my spirits. I felt like I nailed the rest of the pitches that day as well.

For the next two days, I soaked in all the information I could. Anytime somebody offered a business card, I took it without hesitation. During the Q&A session, I asked every question I could think of. I also plowed through the nightly buffets too. I used the rest of the time to roam the streets of Atlanta. Breathing in the city air and seeing the sights and the people gave me ample writing material. I was in my element. More importantly, I didn't feel like my trip was in vain. I thought I made some serious connections, even though I knew they wouldn't pan out right away. Three days in Atlanta would be enough, so I planned to take an early flight home on Sunday instead of Monday.

I couldn't wait to get home and see Essence. Three days without her felt like forever, and I'm sure she would be happy to see me too. I picked up a bouquet of red roses before I went home.

Inside the house, I put the flowers in a vase. Then I thought I heard something upstairs. Essence's car was in the driveway, so I knew she was home.

The farther I got upstairs the more I heard Essence moaning. At first, I was angry because she was pleasuring herself without me. But now that I was there I could join in.

Our bedroom door was cracked, and when I saw her in the doggie-style position getting pounded from the rear, I saw was red. I charged in the room, and Essence and the guy she was fucking jumped off the bed.

"Anthony, I can explain, baby," she said weakly.

"I bet you can, bitch," I said and smirked.

"You need to chill out with the name-calling, boss," the man said as he put on a pair of sweat-pants.

I was so focused on Essence I didn't notice the guy she was fucking was Austin.

I got in his face. "I suggest you step the fuck off."

He put his hands up defensively. "I'm gone. Just tell your girl to hit me up when she need some more of this good dick," he said and grabbed his junk.

Like lightning, I punched him in the jaw, and he staggered back. When he charged at me, I went low and hit him in the kidney.

Essence ran over and grabbed my left arm, but not before I punched him in the face again. He was out cold.

"What did you do?" she yelled.

"What did *I* do?" I asked incredulously. "I beat the shit out of the asshole who fucked my girl!" I yelled so loud my voice cracked.

She got on her knees and grabbed my hands. I couldn't even look at her face. Now she was tainted in my eyes.

"I had a little too much to drink and—"

I cut her off. "I don't want to hear it."

She started crying.

I closed my eyes tight and restrained myself from swinging on her too. "How could you do this to us?" I asked.

"I'm so sorry. I didn't mean to hurt you."

I felt hollow inside. When I looked at Essence, all I saw was a lying and conniving cheater. My heart shattered into a million pieces.

"Lose my fucking number," I said before I stormed off.

I planned to drown myself in vodka to numb the pain.

My world had just crumbled.

September

Waking up at my mother's house and being unemployed sucked. I stunk of failure. I left the nest, and I ended up right back where I started. I had no agent, no girlfriend, and no job. I felt like a piece of shit. I was used to working two jobs, and now I turned into a cliché. I lived in my mother's basement.

I refused to sit on my ass all day, so I went to the unemployment office and got approved for benefits. To be honest, 60 percent of my regular pay beat zero, but my pride hurt more than anything. Paying my bills and having money in my pocket made me feel like a man. If I never had to go back to the unemployment office again and deal with unsupervised kids and their disorganized staff I would be ecstatic.

Although I looked for jobs on Indeed and CareerBuilder, I put most of my focus into my screenwriting. My mother said I could stay at her house until I got back on my feet. I wanted to make sure I was more than good when I left her house for the second time.

At this point, I needed to try to do an independent project to get the attention of Hollywood. Before, I thought that the people would eventually find me, but they didn't.

I had a few brainstorming sessions with my mother, and she told me about her church's young entrepreneur grant program. They gave out the grant twice a year. All I had to do was write a 500-word essay on why I deserved the money.

After I wrote the essay, I scheduled a meeting with Pastor Alex Robinson. I sat in Starbucks waiting for him to show.

I ordered a caramel macchiato and a slice of plain cheesecake while I waited. Ten minutes later, Pastor Robinson coolly strolled in. His cologne made it to the table before he did, and his suit looked tailor-made and expensive. I'm sure his congregation paid for several cleanings to get his teeth that white. He looked more like a movie star than a pastor. When he shook my hand I thought he might rip my arm off.

"Nice to meet you, Anthony," the pastor said and took a seat across from me.

"Nice to meet you too, sir. You want a coffee or a pastry?"

"I'm fine, son, but thank you."

"I appreciate you taking the time to read my essay."

"It was beautifully written. I'm not the only one who has to read it. It has to go through a committee first."

"That's not an issue. I have a detailed business plan if that helps."

"It definitely does," the pastor said and accepted the folder I handed him.

"How long before I know if I got the grant?"

"No more than a week. I will call you personally to let you know which direction we go in."

I stood, and we shook hands. "I appreciate the time, sir."

"No problem, son, and good luck."

I finished my caramel macchiato and sat there long after the pastor left Starbucks. Out of the blue, Essence sent me a text message.

Can we talk?

I replied back: Fuck off!

I had more important things to worry about.

September

I got a letter in the mail denying me the grant. Pastor Robinson didn't even have the decency to give me a call telling me about the bad news. I thought I put together a solid business plan, but obviously, in the committee's eyes, I didn't.

Screw 'em.

Two days later, I put plan B into motion. With the same business plan I used for the grant, I approached my bank for a loan of $6,000.

I sat in TD Bank tapping my foot and mumbling to myself. The loan officer had to call my name twice because I zoned out for a moment.

"I'm Carson Schwartz, and you are?" the loan officer asked.

"I'm Anthony Porter."

"Is it okay if I call you Anthony?"

"Of course."

We sat down at his desk.

"Thank you for submitting your application online. That cuts down on time for us."

"No problem, sir."

"From what I saw, your debt to income ratio is right where we need it to be. It actually exceeds the norm. Very impressive."

I smiled because I took my good credit very seriously, and now it was paying off.

"If it was up to me, I would do it right now, but I have to run this by my manager. Let me print out your file and have a quick chat with him. If everything checks out, the money will be deposited into your account before you leave today."

"Sounds good to me."

The miniature bottle of vodka I drank in the bathroom earlier did little to settle my nerves. Those thirteen minutes I waited for the loan officer to come back felt like an eternity.

When Carson came back over to the desk, his face was emotionless. I was on pins and needles.

"Well, Anthony, my manager is very impressed with your file as well and the $6,000 has been deposited into your account. Congratulations."

I jumped out of my seat and shook Carson's hand with both of my hands because I was so excited. "Thank you, sir!"

A week later, I rented a small, little used nightclub on Columbus Boulevard for three hours. I decided on a forty-five-minute run time to control the cost.

Through Google and YouTube, I found amateur actors who needed acting roles for their portfolio. They understood I couldn't pay them very much money, but they still agreed to do the movie anyway. Luckily for me, I even found someone experienced to shoot the film for us.

Despite having to deal with being unemployed, Essence's cheating, and striking out at first with funding, I actually was going to shoot a movie myself.

It felt really fucking good.

October

The film took a month to complete. Two weeks on shooting. Two weeks on the editing.

Holding a copy of my movie felt surreal.

I had visions of the movie being in Redbox machines across the country. The way I felt, it could've been in just one Redbox machine, and I would've been cool with it. I took a step forward instead of taking one backward, all the damn time.

I blindly sent copies of the film to film bloggers, magazine editors, film critics, and newspaper editors. They had no obligation to respond to any of my inquiries, but I guess I was looking for a miracle.

This film validated all the hard work that I put in. All the bus rides and flights. All the money I spent, and the heartache I experienced brought me to this point. The point of no return. I could only go up from here. I had my hand on the steering wheel, and I dictated the direction. I would force the world to feel my vision.

I put the project up for sale through Vimeo and promoted the movie through social networking and word of mouth. I really felt like the project had some legs. At minimum, the film represented a chance for people to finally see my creativity and for me to get my name out there on some level. Exposure was everything.

I negotiated a sweet deal with TLA on South Street for them to host my movie premiere. We agreed on a sixty–forty split in their favor. I didn't care as long as I got paid. Organically, *Philadelphia* magazine showed up and interviewed me. Apparently, the movie had made a little noise on social media.

After I finished with the interview, Paul walked up on me. We gave each other dap and a hug. We wore rented ivory-colored suits for the occasion.

"Look at all of this." Paul waved his arm toward the people lined up to go inside of TLA. "I'm superproud of you, bro. You came a long way."

"Thank you, man." I became choked up. "I can't believe this is happening."

"I can. This is what happens when hard work and talent meet up."

I nodded and smiled.

"Let's go in here and enjoy the show," I said.

Paul and I filed into TLA behind the crowd.

The theater could hold up to 800 people, and we sold 500 tickets. I couldn't have been happier.

To celebrate making a profit, Paul and I went to Copabanana a few doors down from TLA.

We split a couple pitchers of margaritas and ordered appetizers. It was good to laugh and joke and be carefree. Lord knows I needed to have a good time for a change.

I raised my glass for a toast. "To continued success in the movie biz," I said and smiled.

"To continued success in the movie biz," Paul repeated after me.

October

My luck turned around toward the end of the month. An unknown number popped up on my phone, and I still answered the call with enthusiasm. The caller told me to come in for an interview for the mailroom position. My prayers had been answered.

Standing in front of the mirror, I buttoned my dress shirt and straightened my tie. With a smile on my face, I winked at the mirror, grabbed my things, and left for the interview.

The bus ride into University City took half an hour. The female receptionist at the collection agency directed me to a seat along the wall to wait.

I got a good vibe from the place while I sat in the waiting area. I could see myself coming to work there every day and being comfortable.

After a while, a well-dressed, gray-haired white man approached me.

"Anthony?" he said.

"Yes, sir," I said and stood.

"Nice to meet you, son. I'm Roger Tisdale. I'm the mailroom manager here at Crown and Associates."

We shook hands.

"Let me get us some privacy," he said as I followed him on to the elevator, and then into a giant conference room on the second floor of the building.

Once inside the room, he started right in on me. He sat at a huge desk, and I sat across from him.

"Why are you the right person for this position?" He crossed his legs and arms.

"I'm trustworthy, loyal, adaptive, and interested in working in a team environment."

"Besides money, what's your motivation for working here?" he twirled a pen in his fingers.

"I want to grow with the company." I made sure to look him directly in the eye.

He nodded. "What if I picked someone for the job already and this is a mere formality?" He was stone-faced.

I leaned forward in the chair.

"I would thank you for the opportunity and hope my name comes up in a future consideration for the job," I said truthfully.

He smiled and nodded. "Most people give me shit answers to those questions. As you can tell, I'm a bit quirky with my approach. I've been doing this a long time, and it's always important to keep people on their toes. You sense what they're made of when their back is against the wall."

I nodded and smiled too. "Absolutely, sir."

Once he stood, I got up too.

We shook hands again. "We'll be in touch if we want to move forward with you," he said and smiled before he saw me out of the building.

I hoped they felt as good about the interview as I did because I needed this job like yesterday.

November

Mr. Tisdale formally offered me the mailroom clerk position. As soon as I got my offer letter, I cut my unemployment benefits off.

On the first day of work, I got to University City an hour early. Desperately needing a cup of coffee, I stumbled into a local coffee shop around the corner from my job. I decided to give the place a shot. The inside of the café was rustic and smooth jazz played softly.

An attractive woman finished at the counter and went over to the condiment table. For a brief moment, we locked eyes, and I turned away. I stood there in a daze until the barista called me because I was next in line.

"Sir, what can I get for you?" he asked.

"I'll take a vanilla iced coffee with six sugars and seven creams."

"Coming right up."

Once he handed me the coffee, I ran outside the café and saw the woman about to get into a black Jeep Grand Cherokee. I had no idea what the hell had gotten into me.

"Hey. Hold up a minute." I jogged halfway up the block to catch up with her.

When I caught up to her, she closed the truck door and faced me.

She stood five-four, dark chocolate, thick, gigantic breasts, with short, curly hair.

"Can I help you with something?" she asked with a hand on her hip with much attitude. She looked even sexier with her mad face on.

My relationship with Essence was over, and I was feeling bold. "I'll take your number, but we can start with your name."

She cracked a smile. "Wow. You young boys are so bold these days."

"Young?" I smiled slyly. "How old do I look?"

"You probably still get carded in the liquor store, don't you?" She pinched my cheek.

"Yeah, I do." We shook hands. "I'm Anthony, by the way."

"I'm Mia."

"Nice to meet you, Mia."

"You as well."

I held her hand a little longer than I should have.

"I have to get to work, but I'd like for us to talk again," I said.

"Me too." She handed me her business card. "Don't wait too long to use that, handsome."

"I won't," I said admiring her chunky ass when she turned around.

She got into her truck and pulled out of the parking spot.

I couldn't stop smiling.

Feeling giddy, I walked to my job and took the elevator to the basement.

Mia and I needed to get better acquainted.

Sooner rather than later.

November

Lately, Mia dominated my thoughts. Everything from her gigantic breasts, bright smile, chocolate skin, to her perfect lips. From the moment I met her, she had my head spinning. I wasn't tied to Essence anymore, and I could play the field if I wanted to.

Although I had only known Mia for two weeks, it felt like I knew her longer. We spent hours talking on the phone. Most of our conversations was surface-level stuff, but it still felt good to hear her voice. The next thing on my agenda was to ask Mia out. I wanted to take it slow with her because I thought she was worth the time.

When Michael and my mother fell asleep, I made me a drink and turned on Netflix in the living room. I loved the sound of the rain beating against the window. Just as I hit play on the movie *In Too Deep,* my text message alert went off.

It was a text message from Essence:

Can you open the door?

I replied back: What door?

She said: Your front door.

I knew she couldn't really be standing at my mother's front door in the rain 10:30 at night.

Sure enough, when I opened the door, there she stood with a raincoat on looking sexy as fuck. I looked around quickly before I pulled her inside and closed the door quietly.

"What are you doing here?" I asked.

She touched my face. "I miss you, and you won't respond to my phone calls or text messages."

"You cheated on me, or did you forget?" I asked harshly.

Like lightning, she undid my belt buckle.

"Look, Essence, I don't have time to bullshit with you," I tried to sound stern, but I couldn't concentrate while she stroked me up and down.

"Seriously, I'm not playing with you."

"Shhh," she said and put her finger on my lips. We locked eyes, and she kissed me. Her hands were everywhere at once. She bit my neck and my earlobe. She knew all my sweet spots. I didn't want this to be about sex, but she obviously did. I was at her command. Everything in my brain told me not to get sucked up in her sexual vortex. Everything in my pants said the direct opposite of what my brain yelled.

Her perfume kept me at attention, and her kisses had me breathing heavy with weak knees. Soon enough, we were down in the basement butt-naked.

I ripped her lavender-colored thong off and licked her from her neck to her feet, making sure to stop and suck on her clit. She moaned in delight.

"Put it in," she begged me.

Holding her ankles, I pushed her legs against her shoulders and went inside her raw. Big mistake. Her warmness felt like home. She took it all the way to the hilt as I stretched her insides out with my thickness. I started off slow and then built up speed as I went deeper into the abyss. The sound of our skin smacking together bounced off the walls in the basement. Sweat covered our arms, legs, and foreheads. Every stroke brought me closer to coming. I bit her shoulder it was so damn good.

"I missed you so much, baby," she whispered in my ear.

"I missed you too."

After a few more strokes, we came together, and then snuggled. As soon as we caught our breath, Essence went right in.

"Can we start over?" she asked.

"You cheated on me, and that shit is unforgivable."

Visions of her with Austin almost made me kick her out of the house.

"I made a terrible mistake, Anthony. I beat myself up about it every day. All I'm asking for is one more chance. One more chance to show you how much I'm in love with you." She put her hand on my chest.

I looked in her eyes and tried to find something other than sincerity, but I couldn't. Her words seemed genuine. How could you hate a person and love them in the same breath? It was mind-boggling to me.

"If I see you with him again, you and I are done forever," I said with finality.

"It won't happen again. I promise," she said and grabbed my hand to emphasize her words.

She had some type of hold on me. I hated that I loved her so much. I just hoped she didn't break my heart again, because I don't know if I could take it.

Three days later, I stumbled into the bathroom, and when I went to pee, my dick felt like it was on fire. I immediately called my doctor's office, and they fit me in on a Tuesday.

The next day, I rushed into the office and hoped I got prescribed some strong pain meds. After fifteen minutes of waiting, my doctor came out and we went into an empty exam room.

"What happened, sweetheart?" the doctor asked.

"I tried to pee, and it burned."

She put her hand on my shoulder and gave me a sympathetic look. "Let's run a couple of tests and see what we come up with."

November

The four days I waited for the STD test results were excruciating. Before work, my cell phone rang, and I noticed the doctor's office number on the caller ID. I swallowed hard before I answered the phone as I paced around my bedroom.

"Good morning, Anthony," the doctor said.

"Good morning," I said feeling like nothing would be good about it.

"As you know I'm calling with your test results."

"Yes."

"You have gonorrhea, but it's treatable."

My legs went weak, and I felt like I might throw up.

"How bad is it?"

"You're going to be okay. I sent a prescription to your pharmacy. Take all your medication, and within a week or so, it will be out of your system."

I exhaled the breath I was holding in. "Are you serious?"

"As a heart attack."

"Thank you, Doctor Ross."

"You just be careful next time."

"I will."

She softened the blow somewhat. Although I still planned to choke the life out of Austin and Essence, the news was less deflating. I always had fears of catching an STD. I never thought I would catch one from someone that I loved.

After I got the news, I picked up the prescription at my pharmacy for antibiotics.

Once I got home from work that night, I found out where Austin lived by pulling up the picture I took of his pill bottle at Essence's house.

I made the trip to North Philly.

He lived in a terrible neighborhood that had abandoned houses and people selling drugs out in the open. I got a bad vibe when I got on his block. I spotted his black BMW right away parked in front of a modest-looking home.

As soon as we made eye contact he twisted his face up. Then he got off the steps and approached me. Two guys trailed him.

He blew cigarette smoke in my face. "Talk that shit now."

I looked in all three of their faces before I punched Austin in the jaw, kicked one in the nuts, and rushed the third one. Suddenly, I felt a sharp pain in my shoulder where I got hit with a 40-oz bottle. When I fell to the ground, I curled into a ball to fight off the kicks and punches that rained down on me. If I got the chance to get up, I planned to kick all of their asses.

Luckily for me, police sirens blared in the distance, and Austin and his friends scattered off the block. The police cruiser hopped the curb, and the officers spilled out of the car and helped me to my feet.

"You all right, son?" one of the wide receiver-built officers asked.

"Yes, sir. Thanks for helping me up." I held my sore ribs and winced because of the pain in my shoulder.

"Do you know who did this to you?"

"No."

"You sure?" he asked skeptically.

"I'm sure."

"You need a lift, son?" the officer offered.

"No, thank you, sir. I'm going to catch the bus."

"You be safe out here." He spoke into his shoulder walkie-talkie before getting back into his car.

"I'll try."

I had a few cuts and bruises, but nothing major. My sides were on fire, and I wished I had a chance to go one-on-one with Austin again.

As I sat on the air-conditioned bus, I felt embarrassed. I fought some idiot twice because of a woman worth less than bubblegum on the bottom of my shoe.

Back home, I cleaned myself up with peroxide and cotton balls. I took off my torn T-shirt and lay on my bed. Then I grabbed my phone and sent Essence a text message:

The fact that you gave me a STD is very sad. You need to get yourself checked or you might have known already. Either way, fuck you very much.

I hit send and felt a thousand times better.

Now, I had to be more guarded with my heart than I already was.

December

The gonorrhea wasn't in my system anymore, my job was awesome, people were feeling my movie, and I felt like I was getting closer to Mia. Instead of just surface-level stuff, we got into some personal things.

I told her about my nasty breakup with Essence, and how my agent search was going. She let me know about how she moved here from New Jersey after an abusive relationship and a job change.

I could listen to her talk on the phone all day because her voice was so damn sexy.

Not wanting to waste any more time than I already had, I decided to call her up and ask her out.

I was a little scared, though. What if this led to something? What if I had to put my heart out there again? Was I even ready for that? I threw caution to the wind and dialed her number anyway.

"Hey, you," she said.

"What's up?"

"Nothing. What's up with you?" she asked cheerily.

"Thinking about you." I kept shifting positions on the bed.

"Oh, really? What were you thinking about?"

"How sexy you are."

"Are you getting fresh with me?"

"Yes, I am."

"You better watch your mouth before it gets you into trouble."

"What if I *want* to get into trouble?" I said feeling bold.

"Oh, I can help you."

Things got hot real quick, and I turned the heat down.

"I know we agreed to take things slow, but I wanted to see you again and maybe grab a bite to eat."

"That sounds good to me. What day did you have in mind?"

"How about this Saturday coming up?"

"Well . . . I have a job fair at the Sheraton Hotel in West Philly that day. You can come hang out with me and we can go out after."

"I'm looking forward to seeing you again."
"Me too."

Just thinking about her perfect body and sexy voice turned me on. I couldn't wait to see her Saturday.

December

Saturday came quickly. I spent the first half of the day cleaning the house getting rid of nervous energy. Around 5:00 p.m. that night I stood in the conference room at the job fair waiting for Mia to show up.

Ten minutes later, she came over to me, and I couldn't stop staring and smiling at her. Her breasts looked even bigger, and her pedicure and short skirt were on point.

We hugged, and I didn't want to let go of her.

"Hey, mister. Can you do me a big favor?" she asked.

"Sure."

"Can you go to my truck and get the box off the backseat?"

"Okay." I took her keys, got the box out of her truck, and came back into the job fair.

"Where do you want me to put this?" I asked.

"Over there," Mia said and pointed.

We walked over to a table in the middle of the room.

For the next hour and a half, I watched Mia work her magic with the crowd. She had a natural talent for public speaking and had a magnetic personality. She spoke with so much passion and had the people engaged. I was proud to see her up there doing her thing. People stood around her booth as she talked about the company she worked for and the benefits of working there. The small crowd of people had their choice of what booths they could go to, and they chose hers. Her spiel was believable, and people rushed the table to get applications and business cards. Seeing her in her element made me want her even more.

After the job fair ended, I helped her pack up and put the marketing materials back in her truck.

We ended up at a place called Distrito in University City and sat by the window.

"What do you suggest?" she asked looking at the menu.

"This is my first time here. I found it on the Internet."

She smiled that beautiful smile of hers. "Nothing wrong with trying new things."

"I couldn't agree more." I smiled back.

Mia ordered enchiladas, and I had the carne Kobe tacos. We ate, drank Sangrias, and enjoyed each other's company.

"You did your thing tonight," I said.

"Thank you. I hope we get some good applications."

"I'm sure you guys will."

"I'm glad you asked me out."

"Me too. I just had to see you again."

"I hope we never go that long without seeing each other anymore." She looked me in the eye.

"We won't," I said and reached across the table to touch her hand.

She changed the subject. "How is your agent search coming along?"

"I haven't heard anything yet, but I'm still hopeful."

"They'll contact you. I can feel it."

"I hope so, because this is the only thing I've ever dreamed of doing. I gotta make it big in Hollywood. There literally is nothing else." I slammed my fist into my palm to emphasize my point.

"If I can help in any way, let me know. You speak with the kind of passion that can't be faked. I want to see you make it to the top. Just don't forget the small people when you make it there," she said smiling.

"Those words mean a lot to me. And trust me, you would be hard to forget," I said slickly.

For a moment we stared into each other's eyes. The lustful thoughts running through my head excited the hell out of me.

"I have to get home soon," I said to break the silence.

"You're right. Let's get you out of here, mister." She smiled at me.

Back at my mother's house, she kissed me on the cheek and wiped her lip gloss off my face with her thumb.

"Call me later on," she said.

"I definitely will." I got out of the truck and watched her drive away. Mia intrigued me.

I didn't know if that was a good or a bad thing.

December

I needed to get an old flash drive from Essence's house, and then I would be completely done with her. I was on a mission, and no make-up sex would derail me this time.

I still had a key to her spot, and I was surprised that it actually worked. I assumed she would get the locks changed. I could get in and get out without speaking to her.

Moving as quickly as I could, I found the flash drive in one of the dresser drawers in the bedroom. When I looked around the bedroom, all sorts of emotions hit me like sucker punches. This was the first place where we made love. We held each other in that bed and fell asleep laughing at old *Martin* episodes in that bed. I paid my first real bill in this house. This place was also where she broke my heart. Now it was all up in smoke because Essence couldn't keep her panties on. Just as quickly as I became nostalgic, I kicked the dresser in frustration when I thought about how dirty she did me.

The sound of the front door closing downstairs broke up my memories.

As I came downstairs, Essence looked up at me with her hands on her hips and her head cocked to the side. "What the hell are you doing in my house?"

"I got what I came for, and I'm out," I said and tried to get by her.

She got in my face and blocked my path. "You're a coward to leave me here with all these bills."

"All these bills?" I asked incredulously. "You had these bills *before* I got here. Maybe the food bill went up a little, but nobody told you to get a new car. Your decisions. Your problems. Fuck outta here."

"I needed a real man," she yelled and put her finger in my face. "And that's exactly why I cheated on you."

Her words cut me deep, but I smiled anyway. "Very nice, Essence. Your *real man* gave you gonorrhea, and you gave it to me. So fuck you and your *real man*." I made air quotations.

"Fuck you and your little-ass dick," she shot back.

I busted out laughing at that one. "Don't play yourself. You and I both know the truth. I hope you took your meds. I'm gone."

I went to the front door.

"That's why your dad left you, and your mom is an uneducated bitch," she said and punched me in the back of the head.

Without thinking, I turned around and slapped her in the mouth. When she slammed into the wall, I got scared.

"Shit," I said. I tried to help her up, but she pulled her hand away.

She wiped tears from her eyes and blood from her lip. Seeing that I had hurt her broke my heart into tiny pieces.

She pulled her cell phone out of her pocket.

"What are you doing?" I asked trying not to panic.

"I'm calling the cops on your black ass!" she yelled.

I ran out of her house. I wasn't sticking around for the police to lock me up. I shouldn't have put my hands on her, but I also wasn't trying to go to jail either.

I went straight to my mother's house, and she stood in the kitchen sipping tea. My facial expression must have said it all.

"Let's go in the living room so we can talk," she said.

My mother and I sat on the couch. Images of me hitting Essence flooded my mind.

"Where do I start?" I leaned back on the couch.

She patted me on the hand. "At the beginning, baby."

"I made a terrible mistake today, and I put my hands on Essence."

My mother looked at me shocked. "What happened?"

"It was in the heat of the moment. She hit me first, and I reacted without thinking."

"I don't condone violence against women. You know that. However, I understand mistakes happen. You have to think before you act, son. You hear me?" She grabbed my chin.

"Yes, ma'am."

"What were you over there for?"

"I needed to get an old flash drive."

"She call the cops on you?"

"Yes." I looked at the ground.

"Remember this moment and move on."

"How do I move on and be with another woman after all this drama?"

"If you happen to meet a nice young lady, you take things one step at a time. Go as slow as you possibly can. There is no need to rush."

January

The only bright spots in my life were my mother and Mia. Lately, Mia was in my head a lot. I could smell her perfume, hear her voice, and imagine her touch. I became addicted to her energy.

I needed to see her, so I had her meet me at a hole-in-the-wall sports bar. I figured I could kill two birds with one stone. We could see each other, and she could meet Paul too.

Paul and I sat at the bar nursing drinks.

"Can I still count you in for a donation to the big brother mentorship program?" Paul asked and sipped his beer.

I looked at him like he was crazy. "Of course, man. We can't have them out here with raggedy uniforms."

"I appreciate that. Pretty soon, we'll have enough money to start the basketball tournament."

"Anything I can do to help." I finished my drink and ordered another one.

"I got some good news."

"What's up, bro?" Paul asked.

"Remember the girl Mia I told you about?"

"Of course."

"She's supposed to meet me here tonight."

"It be cool to meet her, bro."

"When she gets here, I'll introduce you guys."

"In the future, please be careful with these women out here. Some of them are full of shit."

"I got my eyes wide open now."

"I just hope this one isn't crazy like the last one."

"Not even close."

"Amen, bro."

Looking like a plus-size model, Mia walked into the bar minutes later. The denim jacket she wore barely held her breasts in place.

When she got to the bar, I got off the stool and hugged her. I brushed against her ass, and she kissed me on the cheek.

"Paul, this is Mia. Mia, this is Paul."

"Nice to meet you, Paul."

"Nice to meet you too, Mia."

They shook hands.

"What are you drinking?" I leaned against the bar.

"I'll take a Malibu Bay Breeze." She reached into her purse.

Grinning, I told her, "Don't embarrass me in front of my boy."

She smiled and closed her bag. Her cell phone rang.

"Can you two excuse me? I gotta take this call." I watched her ass bounce as she walked away.

I waited until she was gone to say something to Paul. "So, what do you think?"

"I can't lie. She is bad," Paul said.

"Didn't I tell you?"

"You did, but do me one favor."

"What's up?"

"If you get into a relationship with Mia, make sure you and Essence are 100 percent done." He patted me on the shoulder.

"Trust me. We're more than done," I said with finality.

"Good shit, bro. You have my blessing." He gave me dap and a hug. "I just want you to be happy. That's all."

"I appreciate you, man."

"No doubt, bro. Let me get up out of here so y'all can chill together. I'm not trying to be the third wheel." He smiled before he left the bar.

Mia came back to the bar and sat next to me just as Paul walked out the door.

"Hey, mister, how have you been?"

"I've been good. You?"

"I've been swamped at work, but other than that, I can't complain." She sipped her drink.

"It's good to see you again."

"The feeling is mutual."

"Let's toast to new opportunities."

We touched glasses, and I swallowed the rest of my drink.

After two more shots of vodka, I almost went into a nod. Mia helped me to her truck.

Half an hour later, we were parked in front of my mother's house.

"I enjoyed hanging out with you tonight," she said.

"I liked hanging out with you too."

I looked into Mia's eyes and licked my lips. Her perfume got me excited. I leaned in, closed my eyes, and kissed her on the lips.

"I'm sorry. I don't know what got into me," I blurted out.

"Don't be sorry." She touched my hand.

I touched her thigh and kissed her neck.

She moaned and grabbed my crotch. Things were spiraling out of control, and I liked living on the edge.

"Can we go to your place?" I nuzzled her neck.

"Yessss," she whispered.

Once we got inside of her condo and had some wine, we were all over each other again. The glasses of wine on top what we drank earlier only pushed things further along.

Her perfume clogged my nostrils, and her lips were so soft. We ended up rolling around on the couch. Our hands were everywhere, and I wanted her so bad I could taste it.

"Wait," I said and sighed. "I can't. Not like this."

"What's wrong?"

"I like you a lot."

She smiled. "I like you too . . . So what's the problem?"

"I want to take my time with you."

"Wow, Anthony. That's very sweet of you."

"I'm sure you're worth the wait." I looked her up and down.

She bit her lip. "Oh, I *will* be."

I couldn't help but smile back. "You want to watch a movie?" I asked.

"Sure. What did you have in mind?"

"Anything without a sex scene."

We watched movies until we couldn't keep our eyes open. Mia fell asleep lying on my chest. I couldn't sleep at all.

On one hand, I was falling for Mia. On the other hand, I didn't want to get played again. I had a tough decision to make.

January

I spent two days at Mia's condo. We went to the movies and dinner, but we didn't have sex. I wanted to, but I also didn't want to rush anything either.

I went back home after work on the second day. A topless Pam Grier was about to serve me brunch before my cell phone's alarm woke me up out of my dream the following morning.

I put on a pair of flip-flops and sat at the computer upstairs. With two tabs open on the computer, I Googled affordable apartments in West Philly, and when I finished searching, I checked my PayPal account. In the last month, I made $700 from my Vimeo sales. I wasn't rich, but it would damn sure help my pockets.

Mia's ringtone went off, and I smiled. Being around her gave me an adrenaline rush. The more I saw her, the happier I felt.

"Hey," I said.

"Hey, mister." She paused. "You weren't busy, were you?"

"Not anymore. I was looking for an apartment I can actually afford."

"Maybe I can help you."

"How so."

"I have a girlfriend who can show you some apartments if I ask her. She owes me a favor."

"I appreciate that. Anything to speed up the process." I wanted to jump up and down I was so excited.

"Let me make a phone call, and I'll come get you in an hour," she said before we hung up with each other.

Mia pulled up outside my mother's house exactly an hour later. When I hopped in her truck, she kissed me on the cheek. I wanted to rip her clothes off and do her right there in the truck. The sexual tension between us hung in the air. It was only a matter of time before one of us made a move.

The first four apartments we visited didn't move me at all. Finally, we drove to a red brick apartment building in West Philly near the college campuses in University City. The block was clean and quiet. Mia's girlfriend reeled me in.

"This unit boasts wall-to-wall carpeting, two bedrooms, one and a half bathrooms, and a washer/dryer combo."

"How much is this going to cost me?" I asked, anxious to get this process over and done with.

"The rent will normally be $900, but with the security deposit included, the payment will be $1,800, Mr. Porter," she said.

This was a big moment for me. The place was close to my job and wouldn't set me back too much. I didn't want to dip into my savings, but I had to make that sacrifice.

"I'll take it," I said and smiled.

"You won't be disappointed." The woman shook my hand and handed me paperwork to sign.

I handed her the signed paperwork and a check, and she handed me the apartment keys. Then Mia and I left the apartment.

"I appreciate your help, Mia." I hugged her.

"You're welcome, mister."

"Let me take you to dinner tomorrow night as a thank you."

"That would be nice."

"Can you come and get me around eight?"

"I'll be there."

"Cool. You mind dropping me at home?"

"Sure thing."

Before Mia dropped me off, I thought about her meeting my mother. Then I thought about when my mother met Essence, and I dropped the idea. I couldn't play myself twice.

My mother was sitting on the couch watching TV and sipping tea when I came in.

"Hey, baby."

"Hey, Mom."

"What's got you smiling so hard?"

"I found an apartment today."

My mother's face lit up, and she jumped off the couch. "Congratulations, baby. I'm so happy for you. When are you moving in?" She hugged me.

"Next month."

"Where is it located?"

"Near University City."

"Okay. That's a pretty good neighborhood."

"Yeah, it is. And I appreciate you letting me stay here for the time being."

"Not a problem at all, baby."

I kissed her on the cheek. "I'm going to bed. I'll see you tomorrow morning."

"Good night, and I love you."

"I love you too."

I went to my bedroom and lay down on the bed. I took my phone out and noticed I had a missed call and a voice mail. I called the voice mail.

You have one new message:

"I don't know how to tell you this, but—" Essence paused. *"I'm two months pregnant, and you're the father."*

"What the fuck?" I hung up and called Essence on her cell phone.

"What a pleasant surprise," she said sarcastically.

"I'm just calling to see if you good."

"Why are you acting like you care about me and my baby?"

"I care about our baby," I said sincerely.

"We'll see how much you care when the real responsibility rolls around."

"I'm going to handle my business."

"You talk a good game, so we'll see."

"You need any money?"

"I'm straight, but if I need something you *will* be the first person I call," she said and ended the call.

The reality of my situation hit me like a freight train. A lot of things scared me about being a daddy. Would I became a shitty father? Would Essence try to make my life a living hell? Would I be able to take on added responsibilities?

Only time would tell.

January

I tossed and turned all night thinking about being a father. In the middle of a nightmare, I woke up in a cold sweat with a dry mouth. I rushed into the kitchen for something to drink.

My mother stood at the stove cooking breakfast. I poured myself a glass of orange juice.

"You okay, baby?"

"No." I sat at the kitchen table and drank my orange juice.

She put a plate in front of me and sat down.

"What happened?"

I bit my lip in frustration. "Essence is pregnant."

My mother sighed. "Are you okay?"

"Yeah," I said flatly.

"How far along is she?"

"Two months."

"And she's just now telling you this?"

I nodded again.

"Is she retarded or something?"

"I'm starting to think so."

We laughed, and then I stopped abruptly.

"I'm not ready to be a father."

"I was scared of being a mother when I had you. You'll be fine. I'll help you get through this. Don't worry about a thing."

"You aren't mad at me?"

"No, baby, I'm not mad at you. I know this is a difficult time. I just want to be there for you." She touched my hand supportively.

"Thank you, Mom."

"No problem at all, baby." She hugged me. "Can you do me a favor?"

"Of course. Anything."

"Please strap up next time."

"I definitely will."

Later on that night, I felt a mix of emotions. I was scared of being a father and fighting against the feelings I had for Mia. It was a lot to deal with.

When Mia came to pick me up, she looked amazing. The skirt she wore showed off her thick legs, and the loose-fitting top showed off her huge breasts.

I wore a black button-up shirt, jeans, and a pair of black sneakers. We went to the Copabanana in University City. Happy hour was ten minutes old when we walked in. While holding hands, we made our way through the crowd.

After two drunk people left the bar, we took their seats. I flagged down the bartender.

"A mimosa for her and vodka with no ice for me."

"Be up in a moment, brother," the husky bartender said and was off.

"I definitely need me a drink," I said.

"Who are you telling? I always need one."

When the drinks came, we touched glasses and swallowed them in one gulp.

"I appreciate you being my friend," I said.

"I appreciate you being mine too."

I took a deep breath. "Can I share something with you?"

"Of course." She leaned forward. "What's on your mind?"

"Essence is pregnant."

She shook her head. "Are you all right?"

"No. I'm scared as hell."

She rubbed my back. "Everything will be okay. I'm here if you need my help."

Mia flagged down the bartender for another round of drinks.

We spent the next half hour eating and drinking. After a while, all I could focus on was getting Mia out of her clothes and into bed.

When we finished at the bar, Mia helped me and my drunk ass into her truck. The cold air felt good on my face. The next thing I remembered we were parked in front of my mother's house.

"Anthony?"

"Yes," I said, half-slurring.

"How long are we going to pretend like we don't like each other?"

I fidgeted in my seat. "I never said I didn't like you."

"You never said you did either," she countered.

I sighed. "I like you, but I've been played before, and I'm not trying to go there again."

She grabbed my hand and looked me in the eyes. "I would never hurt you, mister. I just want to be everything Essence couldn't be." She rubbed my leg. "And so much more."

She put her tongue in my mouth, and we kissed passionately.

When I pulled away, I became lightheaded and saw stars.

"Good night, Anthony."

"Good night, Mia." I kissed her one last time.

I stood there and watched her drive off. She was like a drug, and I couldn't wait to take another hit.

February

I couldn't wait to move into my apartment. I didn't have much to move out of my mother's house. Everything fit into one small suitcase and one big suitcase. Other than that, I had a few boxes, but nothing major that had to be transported.

"Is this everything?" Paul asked.

"Yup," I said and smiled.

"Okay." He closed the back door on his truck.

I went on IKEA's Web site, and they had some pretty dope-looking TVs and furniture sets. I had my eyes on a few of their items. Paul drove us to IKEA on Columbus Boulevard, and I became more hyped by the second. I imagined where I would put everything and how it would look once everything was in place.

Paul helped me find a bedroom set, furniture set, kitchen appliances, and a TV. I gave the store clerk the new apartment address and everything would be shipped there for an extra fee, of course.

"I can't wait to move in," I said excitedly when we got back into the truck.

"I can't wait either so I can come over and raid your refrigerator."

"Very funny."

"I'm dead serious."

My phone rang. I noticed it was Mia's girl-friend.

"Hey. Is everything okay?" I asked.

"I'm afraid not. There's a leaky pipe, and you can't move in for another two weeks. I'm so sorry."

The news took some of the wind out of my sails, but I stayed positive.

"No big deal as long as it's two weeks and nothing more."

"That I can promise you. It will be two weeks from today." Her tone went from worried to cheerful.

"You think I can get a discount for my inconvenience?" I asked half-joking/half-seriously.

"I can probably get you a couple hundred dollars refunded. Does that work?"

"Yes, it does."

"I'll be in touch."

"Looking forward to it."

"What happened?" Paul asked.

"I can't move into my apartment for another two weeks."

"Damn, bro. You going to go back to your moms?"

"Unfortunately."

"Don't worry. These two weeks are going to blow by in no time."

"I hope so."

After I moved into my apartment, I bought a black 2002 Ford Explorer from the auction for $1,500. Public transportation was now a thing of the past.

IKEA had no problem changing the delivery date, and I tipped the deliverymen well for how beautifully they set everything up. I actually had my own place with my name on the paperwork. The only thing that could make my situation better was if I found an agent.

I had Mia over to my apartment, and I made us chicken tacos. We never said we were together. We just did stuff couples do. We hung out and went on dates. The only thing we didn't do was have sex. I wanted our first time to be special.

"That smells good. How long before we can eat?" Mia asked.

"About ten more minutes."

"Good, because I'm starving."

"Me too."

Mia went into the bedroom.

I put the stove burner on simmer when I heard someone knocking at the door.

When I opened the door, my mother walked in with a box under her arm. I kissed her on the cheek and took the box from her.

"What are you doing here?" I asked and set the box on the kitchen counter.

"I wanted to surprise you."

"Now is not a good ti—"

Mia came out of the bedroom and said, "You didn't tell me we had company."

"Anthony, who the hell is she?" My mother gave me the side eye and then focused on Mia.

"This is my girlfriend, Mia. Mia, this is my mother, Brenda."

When I said "girlfriend," Mia smiled.

"I'm glad we finally get to meet. Anthony's told me a lot about you." She stuck her hand out.

My mother smirked. "I wish I could say the same. Anthony's told me *nothing* about you." She looked at Mia's hand like she had shit on it.

"We can get to know each other now," Mia said and stood her ground.

"Listen, Anthony, I wish I could stay, but I have to go, baby. I've got more important things to do."

"No, Mom. I need you to stay." I stood firm.

"You know how I feel about you being with older women."

"Yes, I do, but you're prejudging Mia. She's nothing like Essence. Not even close."

"Oh really?" she said, unconvinced.

"That's one of the best things about her."

We all laughed.

"All jokes aside, Ms. Porter, I want the best for Anthony, just like you do. Having your blessing would mean a lot to us. If you're not okay with this, we won't do it."

My mother looked Mia and me in the eyes and sighed. When her shoulders slumped, I saw a glimmer of hope.

"Okay." She gave Mia a handshake and held her hand. "But if you hurt my baby, I'm on your ass."

"Understood," Mia said and smiled.

Just like that, the ice was broken.

"Can we all eat now?" I asked.

"Sure," my mother said.

For a few hours we ate tacos, drank soda, and talked about any and everything. They even bonded over their love for reality television. I wanted no part of that conversation.

"Dinner was great, baby," my mother said. "We have to do this again sometime."

"Yes, we do," I agreed. "And thank you for the slow cooker."

"No problem . . . It was nice to meet you, Mia."

"Likewise."

"You take care of yourself."

"I will." They hugged each other.

My mother and I stepped into the hallway.

"I'm sorry for how I acted earlier."

"You don't have to apologize, Mom."

"The truth is, I'm weary of these little fast-ass women. But I get a good vibe from Mia. I can tell she's intelligent. I just hope Mia's the one that makes you happy."

"Me too." I hugged her. "I love you, Mom."

"I love you too, baby."

I hugged her again before she went to the elevator, and I went back inside the apartment.

"I'm sorry about how my mother acted earlier," I said.

"There's no need to be sorry. She's just protective over you. Any mother would be."

We sat on the couch.

"In her eyes, I'm always going to be little Anthony. I guess I can understand where she's coming from."

"Seeing how messed up in the head Essence was, I'm not even mad at your mother."

I smiled.

"You want a drink?" I asked.

"Sure. What do you have?"

"I have vodka and orange juice."

"Pour me one."

"Coming right up."

I fixed her a drink, and I had vodka straight up.

We laughed, drank, and talked for a while. She was easy to talk to, and she listened. That was one of the sexiest things about her.

After our last drinks, she grabbed my crotch, and I didn't stop her this time. We were way past due at that point.

I touched her too.

"I can't wait anymore. I need you now," Mia said with lust in her eyes, desire in her voice, and aggression in her touch.

As a response, I grabbed her waist as we kissed passionately. I unzipped her dress and took off her bra. Her huge breasts spilled forth, and I sucked on her chocolate nipples like a milk-deprived infant. She threw her head back in ecstasy.

We rushed into the bedroom and as soon as we stepped foot in there, I got naked too. We couldn't keep our hands to ourselves.

"Lie on your stomach," she said to me seductively.

I did as I was told.

When I got on the bed, she massaged my shoulders and went down to my lower back too.

"You like that?" she whispered in my ear.

All I could do was nod.

When she finished massaging me, she got on the bed, took her thong off, and sat on my face. She tasted so sweet.

She rode my face as I tickled her clit with my tongue.

"Yes . . . Yessss, Anthony. Make me come."

Ten minutes later, I put a condom on and stroked her slowly until she begged me to go harder.

Two orgasms later, she was snoring. With her in my arms, I lay awake, unable to sleep. An episode of *Martin* was on where he thought he might be a father. It made me think of being a father myself. What the hell had I gotten myself into?

June

Four months later . . .

Over the last four months of Essence's pregnancy, I communicated with her through text
message. They usually said something along the
lines of, how's the baby doing or are you okay,
and nothing more. I put money to the side so
that when the baby came, Essence wouldn't be
in a financial hole. I decided to be proactive with
fatherhood.

I did my research on the stages of pregnancy,
and by my calculation, Essence would've been
showing. Although we weren't on the best of
terms, I made sure to check up on her from time
to time. She broke my heart, but she was also the
mother of my child.

One day, I went to visit her at her house. She
answered the door, and I smiled proudly when I
saw her full belly.

"Now is not a good time, Anthony," Essence said . . . and looked over her shoulder.

"Is something wrong?" I asked.

Before she could respond, Austin came downstairs eating a bowl of cereal.

"What is this dude doing here?" Austin asked, standing behind Essence.

"I could ask you the same thing."

"I live here now," he said with a smug grin.

"You let this asshole live here now?" I yelled.

I didn't have a claim on her anymore, but he being around her made me uncomfortable.

"Please stop yelling. You're upsetting the baby, and I could go into labor early."

"Yeah, pipe down, my dude," he said and smirked.

"Fuck you!" I yelled and bumped into Essence's stomach by accident. She grabbed her belly and closed her eyes. I tried to console her, but Austin came around her and stood in my way.

She finally opened her eyes back up. "Anthony, I think you need to go."

"But Esse—" I began.

"Now!" she yelled as the tears fell.

I gave Austin one last dirty look before I bounced.

***

After I hit her in the stomach by accident she wouldn't return any of my phone calls or text messages. I just wanted to know that she and the baby were okay. Eventually, I stopped trying to call her. I wouldn't be the cause of any pregnancy complications.

To keep myself in the loop, I parked near her house and watched her. I grabbed the vodka off the passenger seat and took the bottle to the head.

Essence wanted to be surprised by the bay's gender, but I wanted a little boy. I wouldn't mind him being a junior either. I would teach him how to be a man. Despite what Senior did to me and my mom, I would do my best not to let him down.

This particular day, I followed Essence to her doctor's office. I punished the bottle of vodka and read an Alex Cross novel. When she came out of the doctor's office, she went to the King of Prussia Mall.

Essence parked in the parking lot, and I made sure when she parked I kept on driving. Since she moved a little slower due to the pregnancy, I could keep up with her easier.

She talked on her cell phone as she went into the front entrance. I kept my distance, and when she got a few feet inside the mall, I went in after her.

She went to the second floor. She got some jewelry and perfume before she went into Gap Kids.

I walked past the store and sat on a bench two stores down. She left the store twenty minutes later with three bags. Once she got down the escalator and out of sight, I bolted off the bench and burst into the store.

I went up to the counter, and the guy there smiled at me. "How can I help you, sir?"

I leaned in so only he and I could hear the conversation. "My baby mom just came in her. She was the pregnant woman with the blue shirt."

"Okay . . ." he said as his voice trailed off into uncertainty.

"I need to know what she bought."

He looked around cautiously before answering me. "She bought a lot of baby clothes."

"A boy or a girl?"

"A boy," he said and smiled.

My heart swelled with pride, and I couldn't wipe the goofy smile off my face. I would be bringing a piece of me into the world. Someone to carry on my legacy long after I'm gone.

August

Lately, all I could think about was the avalanche of responsibility about to be dumped on me. By my estimation, Essence was due in a month, and time was ticking.

I used the last few months to replenish my savings account. I worked OT at my job, and my Vimeo account was healthy. So money wasn't an issue. I was ready to embrace fatherhood.

The phone reception in the break room at my job sucked, so I missed calls sometimes. I noticed I had an awaiting voice message. It was from Essence:

The baby came a month premature.

Her phone kept going to voice mail when I called her. I called every hospital in Philadelphia until I found her. She checked into CHOP in University City.

My boss gave me permission to leave, and I drove to the hospital like a madman. I didn't care about the speed limit or anybody else on the road. I beeped the horn and went around the slower drivers. The hospital appeared on my right twenty minutes later. I found a parking spot on the street and sprinted inside and up to the front desk.

"Hello, ma'am, my girlfriend is in the maternity ward here. I need to know what room she's in," I said.

"What's her name, sweetheart?"

"Essence Dwyer."

"This your first child?"

"Yes, ma'am."

"Congratulations."

"Thank you," I said, smiling.

She clicked some keys on her computer. "She's in room six B."

Bursting with joy, I sprinted to the elevator and kept pushing the number "6" like I would get upstairs faster. When the doors opened, I zoomed around the corner and went inside the cold hospital room. By the time I got up there, she had already delivered him.

Essence's mother, father, and a few of the hospital staff were there. Ignoring her parents' sharp stares, I stared at the name tag on the bassinet which read: *Tristan*. I wished I had the opportunity to pick his name, but I was just glad he was here and healthy. Nothing else mattered.

I felt the tears, but I wouldn't let her parents see me cry. My hands shook, and I felt jittery. When I saw his pale skin, head of curly hair, and frail body, my heart ached. I wanted to scoop him up and take him home, but I knew I couldn't. I felt powerless and hoped for a speedy recovery so my son could get out of there as quickly as possible.

"So nice of you to join us, Anthony," Essence said as she lay in the hospital bed.

"Maybe if you called me before you delivered him I would've been here." I didn't even notice that I had raised my voice.

Her father stepped in my face. "Don't talk to my daughter like that, you little punk." He jabbed his finger in my chest.

I looked him in his eyes so he knew I wasn't scared. "It would be in your best interest not to put your hands on me."

"Or *what?*" her father challenged me.

"Touch me again and find out."

By this time, Essence's mother grabbed his arm and said, "Not here, Robert."

My baby boy was hooked up to too many fucking tubes to count, and these two idiots wanted to be assholes. I wasn't for it. After I said a prayer over my son I left the room.

When I got in the hallway I sent a group text message to my mother, Mia, and Paul to let them know the baby came.

That was the best day of my life, and I looked forward to the challenges of fatherhood.

September

Tristan stayed in the hospital for a month while they ran tests and monitored his progress.

With a heavy heart and fear of the unknown, I visited him every day he was under the hospital's care. Seeing him hooked up to tubes felt like a punch in the stomach.

For the first three weeks, Essence and I didn't speak to each other until I decided to be the adult in the situation.

I asked her to follow me into the lounge area near the vending machines so we could talk. We sat down in chairs next to each other.

"We need a solid plan for our son," I began.

"I just want you to be an active father in Tristan's life."

"I plan to be, but I'm going to need your help. Just like you're going to need mines."

"I know," she said barely above a whisper.

Sometimes she could tug at my heartstrings so easily.

"Then we need to work together."

She sighed. "Okay. We can work together."

I touched her hand. "I never thought we would end up here."

"Me either."

"From here forward, we'll help each other coparent. Deal?" I asked.

"Deal," she repeated.

We stood, and I pulled her in for a hug.

"And I'm sorry for—"

"Water under the bridge." I cut her off and headed for the elevator.

At the end of the day this wasn't about Essence or me. It was about the well-being of Tristan, and that's where I wanted to keep it at.

As soon as Tristan got out of the hospital, I called Essence, and we agreed to meet at her house so I could see him. Austin wasn't there, and I decided to have Mia come with me for moral support.

"I can't wait for you to see him," I said as I flew through the yellow traffic light.

"I can't wait either."

When we got to Essence's house, I parked across the street.

Mia and I hopped out of the truck and held hands. Just as we got on to Essence's front steps, she answered the door with a smile on her face. When she saw Mia, she immediately grilled her.

"Who's this bitch?" Essence asked.

"You gon' find out if you call me out my name again."

"Listen here, Miss Thi—"

I cut Essence off. "I didn't come here for you to argue with my girl."

"Your girl?" Essence asked in a deflated tone.

"Yes. My girlfriend."

"Why would you bring her here?"

"That's irrelevant. I'm here to see my son."

Essence smiled devilishly. "If you two idiots don't leave right now, I'm calling the cops and telling them y'all tried to jump me."

"Let me give you a reason then," Mia said and lunged for Essence, who moved just in the nick of time.

I decided not to chance it and pulled Mia back toward the truck.

"This ain't over, Essence. I can promise you that," I said.

"*Whatever*, Anthony. Get ready to start paying child support." She slammed her door shut.

"That little girl is lucky I didn't bust her upside the head."

I had a mind to let Mia beat the brakes off Essence.

"I'm going to go at her another way."

"What did you have in mind?"

"I'm going to file for joint custody."

October

While I waited to get the custody paperwork back from the court I did everything in my power to see Tristan. I showed up at Essence's house, and she was never home. One night I actually slept in my truck outside her home. She neither came out nor in. In fact, I never saw the lights in her house go on. I suspected she might have been staying somewhere else, but I had no idea because she wouldn't answer my calls, text messages, or e-mails. I even went by her job, and they told me she was taking time off. I was desperate and at the end of my rope. I didn't know what to do until one day, out of the blue, she called me.

I answered the phone, "About time you called me back."

"You can come and get Tristan."

Not caring why she was letting me see my baby on a random Wednesday night, I eagerly accepted her offer. "I'll be there."

Usually when I went to Essence's house, there was some type of drama associated with my visit. It felt good to be going there under normal circumstances. I wanted to see my boy and that was it.

When I got there, she answered the door with a smile and moved to the side so I could come in. I sat on the couch.

"Make yourself comfortable. You want something to drink? Water? Soda?"

"I'm okay. Thank you." I was all business.

"All right. Give me a minute, and I'll be right back." Essence disappeared upstairs.

I picked up a magazine off the coffee table and flipped through the pages.

Out of nowhere, Essence stood in front of me wearing purple lingerie and way too much perfume.

"What the hell are you doing?" I scooted over to the other end of the couch to avoid her touching me.

She sat next to me. I jumped up to get away from her, and she pinned me against the wall by the wrists. She tried to kiss me on the lips, but I turned away, so she kissed me on the cheek. Her lips on me made my skin crawl and stomach flip. She did nothing for me anymore. I would rather kiss a public toilet seat then to have her touch me ever again.

She tried to grab my crotch, and that's when I broke free and pushed her away.

"Where is he, Essence?" I fell into one of her manipulative traps again. I could've kicked myself for being so stupid.

"Why? I need you to focus on *me*," she yelled with a crazed look in her eyes.

I thought she had mental issues before. I knew for sure now. Frustrated, I ran upstairs to look for Tristan. She was talking, but I ignored her.

I punched the wall when I realized Tristan's room was empty. I rushed back downstairs and got in her face.

"Where the fuck is he?"

"With my parents." She trailed her finger along my shoulder.

I shook my head. "You played me yet again."

"Anthony, if I'm not happy . . ." She put her hands on her hips and craned her neck. ". . . you won't be either."

"You have some serious problems."

"I want you, baby. Your little girlfriend can't do you like I can." She licked her lips.

"I'm here about Tristan. You and I are done."

"If I don't get what I want, then you don't get to see Tristan."

"Why are you playing games like a little fucking kid?"

She shrugged. "Because I can, and there isn't shit you can do about it."

I raised my hand like I would hit her, but thought better of it.

"Go ahead and hit me again. I'll have the cops lock your black ass up!"

"Fuck you." I stormed out of the house and hopped in my truck.

The nerve of her! She flaunted her ass around and expected me to fall in line. I'm sure I bruised her ego by rejecting her like I did.

I needed my court paperwork to go through ASAP.

October

Mia's parents lived in the same Collingswood, New Jersey, home where she grew up after she and her folks moved from Camden. Her parents were having a get-together, and Mia invited me to come. I was scared to meet her mother and father. I hoped they were nothing like Essence's parents.

We parked around the corner from the house and walked the rest of the way.

Once we got inside her parents' place, her dad greeted us first. He bear-hugged Mia and kissed her on the forehead. They looked alike.

"Anthony, it's a pleasure to meet you." We shook hands.

"Likewise, sir."

"Mia can't stop talking about you. Congratulations on fatherhood as well. Children are a blessing."

"Thank you again, sir." I smiled proudly.

Their house was beautiful. Everything looked new and untouched. The place smelled like baby powder. A huge TV was mounted on the wall in the living room, and I could see a bar in the kitchen. Living in a place like theirs would be a dream come true for me.

Mia's mother joined us. I felt terrible for staring. She was bad too, though.

She gave me a warm hug.

"Finally, I get to meet this young man. Oooh, and he's handsome too."

I made the rounds and spoke to everyone in attendance. People were everywhere. Most of them knew of me already because of Mia.

While she played cards with her aunts, I went and got me some food. They had Memphis-style dry rubbed ribs, lemon pepper chicken, buttery corn on the cob, and macaroni salad with bacon in it. I took my plate and an orange soda and sat in the living room.

After I finished with my food, Mia came into her parents' living room and kissed me on the cheek.

"Hey, you."

"Hey."

"You enjoying yourself?"

"Of course. Me and food have a special kind of relationship."

She hit me on the shoulder playfully. "You're too much."

"Your parents are pretty cool."

"I'd like to think so."

"I have to personally thank them for getting it on or you wouldn't be here," I said and kissed her on the shoulder, neck, cheek, and lips.

"Are you getting fresh with me at my parents' house?"

"Yes, I am."

"Just wait until we get back to your place," she said and grabbed my crotch.

After Mia and I quickly said our good-byes, I mashed the gas pedal into the floor.

At my apartment building, we hopped out of the truck, and I got the mail while Mia went upstairs into my apartment.

My hands shook as I opened the envelope and read the letter.

Dear Anthony Porter, I began . . . .

When I finished reading the letter, I rushed upstairs. Now I had a headache.

Mia was in her bra and panties holding a champagne flute. Disappointment was written all over my face. "What happened, baby?"

"That dirty bitch filed for sole custody and negated my paperwork."

November

At 9:45 a.m., Mia and I sat in her truck parked down the street from the courthouse. I sipped on spiked coffee, and she had no idea.

"I hope the mediator is a man. I'm scared a woman will believe Essence's bullshit and side with her," I admitted.

"That's not necessarily true, but I see your logic. I just want an unbiased mediator. I don't care if they're a man, woman, or an alien," Mia said and sipped her orange juice.

"I figured Essence and I could split time with Tristan, and it would be this easy thing." I finished the coffee and put the empty cup in the cup holder.

"It should've been easy. This chick is crazy as cat shit, so I'm not surprised she's being difficult with you."

"I'll be glad when I have something in writing."

"Me too."

"I'm scared she'll try to sabotage me."

"Show the mediator you're ready to take care of your son. Court is about who builds the best argument. Facts be damned. If she can prove you're nonchalant and irresponsible, she wins the battle. Prove her wrong." Her tone was stern but supportive.

Her consistent support warmed my heart. "I still have the receipts from the clothes and diapers I bought him."

"The mediator will see you're serious. The receipts will be proof. He or she will have no choice but to believe you."

I kissed Mia on the lips. "Thank you for riding with me. You're a real woman. I'm disappointed we didn't meet sooner," I smiled.

"We met at the perfect time. God isn't in the mistake business. Never has been. Never will be."

We kissed again before we got out of the truck and walked down the street and into the court-house. It was time to fight for my son.

Essence and her parents were standing in the lobby, and I walked past them like they weren't even there.

I walked into the family court waiting room and noticed the ten chairs and the eggshell-col-ored walls. Although there was plenty of space in the room, I felt claustrophobic. Five of the chairs were taken. Two adults on one side. Two adults and one child on the other. It was surprisingly quiet in there too.

At the intake counter, I signed my name on the clipboard and Mia and I sat down.

Essence and her parents came in minutes later and sat on the other side of the room facing us.

I smiled when my mother and Paul walked in after them. Essence and Mia grilled each other. I let my mother sit down, and Paul and I stood side by side grilling Essence's father.

"Dwyer and Porter," a tall brunette woman with glasses said.

Essence and I got up and followed behind her down a hallway and around a corner. We all sat down in the medium-sized office.

"I'm Nancy, and I'll be handling the case between you two," she said warmly.

Essence and I said hello.

"So, Ms. Dwyer, since you filed your paperwork first, what would you like to accomplish here today?" Nancy asked.

"I want sole custody of my son," she said flatly.

I wanted to yell "our son," but I kept quiet.

"Is there any reason for this request?" Nancy leaned back in her chair and studied Essence.

"I want his visits supervised because I can't trust him."

"And why don't you trust him?" Nancy asked skeptically.

"He hasn't been active in Tristan's life like he's supposed to be," Essence said and folded her arms across her chest.

"Yes, I have, and I can prove it," I cut in and handed Nancy a folder.

She flipped through the contents of the folder. "Well, Ms. Dwyer, from what I can tell, Mr. Porter is gainfully employed and has no criminal record. Mr. Porter also has receipts for baby clothes and phone records that show he's been calling you and texting you. You haven't been very responsive."

When I looked over at Essence, she had the stupidest look on her face.

"Well, he doesn't support us financially either."

Nancy shook her head. "I see here Mr. Porter has written you a check for $1,000. This man wants to see his child. To deny him that would be immature and, quite frankly, it would be stupid."

Essence looked shocked that this woman called her on her shit. I wanted to jump out of my seat and hug Nancy.

"I guess we have to go to court."

"You could do that, but with all of this evidence, the judge would throw out your claim for sole custody. It would be a total waste of your time," Nancy said seriously.

Essence became silent for a moment, and that shocked the hell out of me.

"What do we have to do to get this over with this?" she asked with major attitude.

By the time Essence and I finished in mediation, I got visitation every other Saturday and Sunday. Essence gave me all her contact information, including her phone number, address, and e-mail address. I almost broke down and cried in Nancy's office I was so happy.

Afterward, Paul, Mia, my mother, and I went out to Olive Garden for a celebratory dinner. A huge weight shifted off of my shoulders.

I went through a two-week probationary period before I had my first visit with Tristan. Essence and I agreed on a time for me to pick him up the day my probation ended. Just to make sure she was home on the day I was to pick Tristan up, I called her cell phone. An automated voice told me, "The number you dialed is currently not in service."

That struck me as odd.

Her house phone gave me the same message. I wondered why she changed both her numbers and didn't bother to tell me. Something felt off.

Ignoring the speed limit and the stop signs, I got to her place in record time. Her truck wasn't parked in the driveway.

I got out of my truck and rang the doorbell. When that didn't work, I banged on the door and yelled her name. She didn't respond, so I looked through her windows.

The living room was empty.

My heart shattered into a million pieces, and my breaths became short and ragged. I kicked the trash cans over and threw the baby bag at the wall.

I took a few moments to get myself together before I drove to Mia's condo. I wanted to hurt Essence so bad I could feel it in my bones. A half hour later, I parked on Mia's block and then went into her building.

Feeling dead inside, I plopped down on the couch when I got inside her place.

"Is everything all right? Where's Tristan?" Mia asked.

"Essence played me," I said and put my head down.

"What happened?"

"I went to get him, and she wasn't there."

"You mean, like, not home?"

"No. She moved out of the house, and I don't know where they are."

Mia shook her head and folded her arms.

"I hoped she would stop playing games. Especially after you guys went to court. Obviously, she couldn't do that."

"The gloves are off now. This bitch started a war."

November

I sat at my kitchen table drinking vodka from the bottle. Tristan had been gone for three days, and the alcohol numbed me to reality. I called out of work the last three days too. My life fell apart.

The police did the best they could do to help me. I gave them all the information I had on Essence. Her date of birth and her work address. I didn't know any of her girlfriends' addresses or phone numbers. I also filed a missing person's report and came up with nothing.

My worst fear had come true. She took my son and disappeared, and I couldn't find her. I felt powerless because no one could help me out of my situation. According to the police, she hadn't used her credit card or cell phone in the last few days. They told me they would call me if they found out anything of note to report.

I was angry, scared, and frustrated. With the vodka bottle tucked under my arm, I hopped in my truck and drove to Essence's job.

I parked across the street from her job and waited for her to show up.

After waiting for an hour, I hopped out of the truck and burst through the front doors and walked up to the receptionist.

"Hello, sir. How can I help you?" she asked me and smiled.

"I need to speak with Essence Dwyer, please," I said and smiled back.

"Your name?"

"Anthony Porter."

"One moment, sir."

"Thank you."

I sat down in the lobby and read a magazine while I waited.

The receptionist called me back over to her.

"Ms. Dwyer is no longer an employee at this office."

"What do you mean she's no longer an employee at this office?" I slapped the counter.

"I apologize for the inconvenience." She fidgeted in her seat like a small child.

"This is bullshit. Do you at least have her new work address?"

"I can't give out that information."

"Of course you can't," I said sarcastically. "Am I listed as her emergency contact?"

"Again, I'm sorry."

"Thanks for nothing."

I kicked a chair before I left. When I got in my truck, I punched the steering wheel over and over again. Then I went to Essence's parents' house. I rang the doorbell, and her mother answered.

"Anthony, what are you doing?" she whispered. She looked surprised and scared.

Her husband appeared out of nowhere. "What the hell do you want? You got a lot of damn balls coming to my home without an invite."

I ignored him. "Is Essence here?"

"Go inside, sweetheart. I'll take care of this. It won't take me long."

He closed the front door, walked up on me, and poked me in the chest. "Why should I tell you anything?" His nostrils flared when he talked.

I held my anger in check.

"I don't mean any disrespect, sir. She took Tristan, and I don't know where they are."

"I'm going to tell you this one time, Anthony. You come to my house again, and I won't guarantee your safety." He cracked his knuckles.

"Are you threatening me, sir?" I asked in disbelief.

"I skip the threats, son. I go straight to promises. Test me if you want to."

I smirked. "I'm supposed to be scared of you, huh?"

He smirked back. "She told me about your little drinking problem." He folded his arms. "And if you put your hands on my daughter and grandson again, I'm going to put my foot in your narrow ass."

"What? She's lying to you. I would never—"

He cut me off.

"Abusive and a drunk, huh? Get off my property, you sorry piece of garbage," he said and went into the house.

Essence wanted to destroy my character. All I wanted to do was be a good father to Tristan. What the hell happened to us?

After I left her parents' house, I went straight to the courthouse to file modification of visitation paperwork. Without a home or work address, they told me she couldn't be served. I ran into yet another brick wall.

Feeling depressed, I drank the rest of the vodka from the bottle and headed home and openly ignored the speed limit and stop signs.

Suddenly, a cop appeared out of thin air and signaled for me to pull over.

"Fuck," I yelled.

When the cop came up to my window, I rolled my driver's side window down.

"What's the problem, Officer?"

He didn't respond. He looked around the truck stone-faced before he said, "License and registration."

November

When the cop pulled me over, I thought I would shit on myself. I had vodka on my breath and a liquor bottle on my passenger seat. Basically, I was fucked.

I drove drunk before, but I never got caught slipping. On top of arresting me, they impounded my truck too.

Because of the DUI arrest, I had to take a breath, blood, and urine test and, unsurprisingly, I failed every one. Being stuck in a mildew-smelling cell, only being able to eat dry cheese sandwiches, and being stripped of my freedom sobered me up real quick. I never wanted to see a bottle of vodka again in my life. I just wanted to go home.

For those two days in lockup, I thought of everything under the sun. One of the most important things being that I was in denial about my drinking. I justified that it was okay if nobody got hurt, but that was bullshit. I could've very well gotten into an accident, and it would have been 100 percent my fault. I was the one with the alcohol in my system. What would have happened if the cop didn't pull me over?

I didn't want to be this kind of man. A man that couldn't make adult decisions. The kind of man that was reckless and could have endangered the lives of innocent people. The kind of man that can't hold his liquor.

I lay on that uncomfortable bed feeling embarrassed. My mother brought me up to be a levelheaded individual, and I shitted all over that guidance with the boneheaded decision I made.

Being a young black male, I knew that in some circles I was expected to be a criminal or in jail, and all I did was feed into the stereotype. I saw a sea of different colored people in lockup, and I knew I didn't belong there. Maybe some of them didn't belong there either.

It shattered my heart when I heard the disappointment in my mother's voice. I was always a closeted alcoholic, and to have to reveal my addiction made me feel less than shit. I know she supported me, but I knew this put a strain on her heart that I never wanted to be there.

There was no telling how Paul and Mia would look at me. I hoped they would support me through my rough patch. I vowed to hit the straight path because I never wanted to see the inside of a jail cell ever again. There is nothing cool about being locked up. I had to man up, and this DUI let me know that my freedom is precious. I wouldn't do anything like this again to jeopardize my future.

Liquor and I had officially broken up. Vodka proved to be a crutch, and it was time to stand on my own two feet.

Like a grown man.

When I got out of lockup two days later, I was happy to see Mia parked outside waiting for me. Although it was only forty-eight hours, I felt like a changed man.

I couldn't get down the steps fast enough when I saw her get out of the truck. When I went in for a hug, she stepped back and punched me in the shoulder.

She finally let me hug her but continued to hit me in the chest as I held her.

"I'm sorry," I whispered in her ear.

"You could've been in an accident or worse—"

I cut her off. "I made a mistake, and I promise I won't do it again."

"You better not. Because I'll kill you my damn self."

***

That's how my secret got out. I had an in-depth conversation with Mia and Paul. They didn't judge me about my drinking problem. They agreed to help me get rid of my demons. The first step was admitting I had a problem, and I planned on getting the help I needed. When vodka starting effecting my life negatively, I knew trouble would be ahead.

My driver's license would be suspended for two months. For the time being, I would be back on public transportation. On top of that, I had to do 150 hours of community service.

I turned my focus back on finding Tristan. I took the bus to Essence's old neighborhood. When I got there, I noticed her mailbox over-stuffed with mail.

As I looked through her mail, her next-door neighbor came outside. When I saw him, I put the mail back in the mailbox.

"Anthony? What are you doing here?" he asked suspiciously.

"I need your help."

"Sure thing. What do you need?"

"Essence been by here lately?"

"I haven't seen her. She up and left and hasn't been back here since."

"Were you home when she moved out?"

"Yes. She and some guy packed everything into a U-Haul van and disappeared."

All I could think about was Austin being around my son. I wanted to break his jaw on sight.

"Did she say where they were going?"

"No, she didn't." He paused like he had remembered something else. "But the man she was with had New Jersey license plates. I don't know if that helps."

I nodded. "Actually, it does."

December

When I wasn't at work or looking for Tristan I was promoting my movie through the Internet and by handing out business cards. The promotion had a noticeable impact because every week, the viewership numbers jumped up several thousand. Now all I had to do was parlay that into getting me an agent.

After work, I sat on the couch, on Mia's laptop, searching for Essence's address through a Web site called Findaperson.com. Five results popped up, but none in New Jersey. And her old address showed up too.

Two of the people's names had the wrong middle initial. The last two people had the right middle initial but had P.O. boxes for the address.

When I Googled every address one by one, I came up with a bunch of disconnected numbers associated with them. On top of this, the people at the post office refused to help me. I know they were only doing their job, but I was still pissed off about it.

I went down another dead end.

Needing to get my mind off the nonsense, I called Mia's cell phone.

"Hey, mister."

"Hey, sugar mama."

"What were you up to?"

"Nothing much."

"How was work?"

"They still pay me, so it was beautiful."

"You are aware that there's something wrong with you, right?"

"But that's why you love me."

"Maybe just a little."

"You want some company?"

"Don't threaten me with a good time."

An hour later, Mia and I were eating extra butter microwave popcorn and watching a Lifetime movie. I hated watching love stories, but she loved romance, so I tolerated them because of her. I always appreciated quality time with her.

Halfway through the movie, Mia rubbed my leg all the way up to my crotch. As soon as I rubbed on her breasts, my cell phone rang and interrupted our moment. I didn't recognize the number, but I picked up anyway.

"May I speak to Anthony Porter, please?" the caller asked.

"Speaking."

"I'm Anderson Vegas with the Vegas film agency. You have a minute?"

My heart beat sped up. "Absolutely."

"I bought a copy of your movie, and I was very impressed. I would very much like to represent you."

His words didn't register with me right away. Somebody had to be playing a trick on me, right?

"Anthony, you still there?" he asked.

"I'm here, but I'm trying to figure out if you're serious."

He laughed. "I'll do you one better. In about five minutes check your e-mail. It will have a link to my Web site and a copy of the agent-screen-writer agreement. If you like what you see, give me a call back on this number. Cool?"

"Cool."

"We'll talk again soon," he said confidently.

I disconnected the call.

"Who was that?" Mia asked.

"It was an agent. He wants to represent me."

She smiled. "That's good news, right?"

"Somebody is playing a trick on me." I was in utter disbelief.

She shook her head. "Does the agent have a Web site?"

"He does, and I'm going to check it out now."

I waited five minutes and checked the e-mail on my cell phone. I followed the link and looked through his client list and read the testimonials. His track record was solid, and his clients seemed to love him.

Anderson also had a degree in marketing and communication. So far so good. Then I checked out the agent-screenwriter agreement. The agreement stated that he had ninety days to get me an offer. If in ninety days I didn't have any offers on the table, I could terminate our partnership.

I turned to Mia and smiled like the Cheshire cat. "He's official!" I yelled at the top of my lungs.

Mia and I hugged and kissed. "I knew you could do it. I'm so damn proud of you."

"Thank you. Thank you for being there and believing in me. Now I gotta tell Paul and my mom the good news."

"You have to tell them tomorrow," she said.

"Why?"

"Because you're going to be busy for the rest of the night."

"With what?"

"With me," she said and pulled her shirt over her head and unhooked her bra.

December

Through an exhaustive Google search, I found a private investigator named William Dean out of Villanova, Pennsylvania. We had a phone conversation, and he laid everything out for me. He would cost me twenty-five hundred. He wanted half up front and the other half when he found Essence. I refused to play games with her anymore.

I was short on the twenty-five hundred, and I didn't get paid for another two weeks to cover the rest. I didn't want to ask Mia, Paul, or my mother for the money, so I was forced to wait until I could pay.

In the meantime, I still tried to find Essence on my own. I struck gold when I found a Web site that advocated for fathers' rights. They even had an Android app I could use. From the testimonials posted on their Web site, they looked decent and they were free, so I gave them a try. I didn't have much to lose at that point.

I spoke with a man named Scott Taylor, and from the moment I got on the phone with him, I felt comforted. He told me to send him any personal information I had on Essence and all of our court paperwork. While we were on the phone, I scanned and e-mailed everything to him.

Three weeks after we spoke, Scott had an address for Essence somewhere in South Philly. He was that good.

I went out and bought Tristan new clothes, diapers, and baby toys. I put everything in the trunk of my truck and used my GPS to get to her apartment.

As I pulled off, I called Mia on her cell phone.

"The fathers' advocate people gave me a working address on Essence somewhere in South Philly."

"Good, but don't do anything that could come back to hurt you in court," she said cautiously.

"I'll try, but I can't make any promises. Especially if her little boyfriend is there," I said truthfully.

"Let's hope he isn't there and you can see Tristan."

"I'll call you on my way back. I love you."

"I love you too."

I got to Essence's apartment building and parked across the street from the crappy-looking red brick building. Garbage lay on the sidewalk, and abandoned buildings made up most of both sides of the street.

I shook my head and wondered why Essence lived there. I could care less about her, but I didn't want Tristan living in a bad neighborhood.

When I got out of my truck, I saw her car parked ahead of me on the same side of the street.

As I got to the door of her apartment building, someone walked out. I slipped inside before the door closed. The overweight black woman looked at me funny but didn't say anything.

The hallway smelled like old cooking oil and Gain fabric softener sheets. I ran up two flights of stairs and went to apartment 301.

My face felt hot, and my nerves were rattled as I knocked on the door.

A few minutes passed, and nobody answered. I banged on the door until someone came out of another apartment.

"Are you looking for Essence, young man?" an old woman in a raggedy pink housecoat asked me. A cigarette hung from her thin lips. She tapped the cigarette, and ash fell on the carpet.

"Yes, ma'am, I am." Desperation coated my voice.

She shook her head. "You're that boy's father, aren't you?"

"I am. How did you know?"

She blew out a cloud of smoke. "He looks just like you," she smiled.

"Have you seen them lately? Him and his mother, I mean."

She let ash fall again and wore a look of sadness. "She sold her car to someone in the building and moved out about a week ago."

January

Every day after I came home from work and doing my community service, I got on the laptop and searched the Internet trying to find Essence's new address. I didn't get very far. A couple of times I almost threw the laptop at the wall, I was so frustrated with the whole process.

When I got my next paycheck, I met the private investigator, William Dean, at his Villanova office. The place wasn't much to look at and was located on a nondescript side street. A suit-clad Mr. Dean greeted me at the door, and we went and sat in his small office.

"How did you find her?" I asked eagerly.

"I have a lot of helpful contacts. The most important being at the DMV and the Social Security office. Ms. Dwyer registered her Mercedes-Benz in the state of New Jersey, and she got a replacement copy of her Social Security card. Her previous address and place of employment really helped me too. I also have some other methods I can't divulge to you."

"As long as you got the job done I don't care." I smiled and handed him the rest of the money I owed him.

I decided to pay Essence a surprise visit and used GPS on my phone to get to her house.

She lived in Moorestown, New Jersey. I couldn't front on how nice the three-story red brick single-family home looked. The tree-lined neighborhood was low-key with a few luxury cars parked in front of a bunch of modest-looking homes. I parked across the street a few doors down so she wouldn't see me.

She came outside holding Tristan around 8:00 a.m. that morning. Seeing him up close for the first time in a while warmed my heart.

I watched her strap him in his car seat, get in the car, and pull off. I hoped we would be in court soon so the court could put an end to her nonsense.

She drove past me, and I followed her. Her first stop was a day care not too far from her house. I typed the address into my cell phone and saved the information.

She came back outside quickly, hopped back into her car, and got on the highway. I followed her all the way to her job and parked in her parking lot. Then I waited for her to walk inside the office building before I started the truck back up.

Since I had her work and home address, I could finally file paperwork for us to go back to court. What would happen from there was anybody's guess.

"Got you, bitch," I said to myself and peeled off out of her parking lot.

February

I believed my agent when he said he was still putting feelers out for my work, but the results weren't there. I wasn't the most patient person in the world, and I wanted things quicker than the average person. On top of that, Essence still hadn't been served with the court paperwork. I wanted to hit the liquor bottle so badly.

The monkey clawed at my back as I thought about the familiar tingling sensation on my taste buds when I drank vodka. When I closed my eyes, I could smell the liquor. I searched all through my cabinets and all my hiding spots and came up empty. I moved so fast throughout my apartment that I started sweating. When I didn't find anything, I kicked the dresser in my bedroom in frustration.

I caught a glimpse of myself in the mirror and came away disappointed. Here I was, acting like a junkie looking for my next fix. Memories of being in jail for two days flooded my mind and how I would look to my peoples falling off the wagon. I couldn't disappoint them again. I wouldn't disappoint them again. Even though the temptation grabbed ahold of me, I broke free because I had to be the man Mia needed me to be. Being weak wasn't an option.

To keep my mind off of drinking vodka, I set up a romantic evening with Mia. I made dry rubbed rib-eye steaks, sautéed asparagus, Caesar salad, and crab-stuffed shrimp.

I cleaned my entire apartment, lit some lavender-scented candles, and put on some old-school R&B. I wanted the night to be perfect.

After digging through my bedroom closet, I picked out a white dress shirt, black slacks, square-toed shoes, tie, and a stylish belt.

Then I put a tablecloth on the table with plates, glasses, and silverware.

Mia walked in the house, and I hugged her and inhaled the sweet scent of her perfume.

"What are you up to?" she asked with a raised eyebrow.

"Just a little something for my lady."

I grabbed her hand and went into the dining room.

"Everything looks beautiful, Anthony."

"It's all for you," I smiled. "Just wait until you taste the food."

I pulled out her chair at the dining-room table.

"Thank you, mister," she said and smiled.

"My pleasure."

I poured us each a glass of iced tea and started the microwave. Once the microwave stopped, I put the plates on the table and sat down with Mia.

"I made this dinner just to say I love you and I appreciate you." I touched her hand.

"I love and appreciate you too."

"Now let's dig in," I said and grabbed my fork.

"Let's."

After dinner, I ran Mia a bubble bath and put lit candles around the bathroom.

Seeing her naked in bathwater up to her breasts, I almost jumped in the water with my clothes on.

Her shadow played on the tiles behind her. She was sexy without trying.

On my knees, I washed her from her neck to her feet. She closed her eyes and bit her lip. Seeing her excited made me excited.

After I finished bathing her, I helped her out of the water and gave her a towel to dry off with. The candlelight in the bathroom made her skin glow.

From the doorway of the bedroom, I watched her get dressed after she dried off. She slipped on a black negligée and a pair of black high heels. She kept a few sets of clothes at my apartment, and I was glad she did.

She looked amazing.

Before she could say anything, I kissed her on the mouth.

With her back to me, I massaged her shoulders. I loved how her skin felt against mine.

"Lie on your stomach," I whispered in her ear and licked her earlobe.

She did as she was told.

I took my clothes off and joined her.

February

When I got home from work, the first thing I did was check my mailbox. I had two pieces of mail. One envelope was from a payday loan place they just built near my apartment building. The other envelope was from the family court.

I rushed upstairs into my apartment and opened the other envelope. Once I read over the letter, I laughed.

Once again, she filed paperwork before me and had me summoned to court for sole custody. Even when I was proactive, she still beat me to the punch. Despite that, I was more than ready to battle with her in court. I missed Tristan so much, and I didn't want to waste any more time.

My cell phone vibrated in my pocket and interrupted my thoughts.

"Hey, Anderson, what's up?" I said as I paced around my living room. I hoped he had good news for me because I damn sure needed to hear some.

"I'm calling to tell you I'm a man of my word. I got some good news for you."

My hands wouldn't stop shaking. "Okay, I'm listening."

"I spoke with Paula Stevens at Dynamite Entertainment, and—" I cut him off in midsentence.

"Did you just say Dynamite Entertainment?" I was in total disbelief. They were only the biggest independent film company in the movie business.

"Yes, I did, and I'll cut right to the chase. I negotiated a deal for them to buy *Compromised* for $150,000," he said excitedly.

"A hundred and fifty thousand dollars?" I repeated to make sure I heard him correctly.

"Yup."

I broke out into a silly dance and screamed "Yes" at the top of my lungs. "Do I get all the money at once?" I asked when I put the phone back to my ear. My heart was beating double time.

He laughed. "No. You'll get the money divided up into four payments. Once you sign the paperwork, I'll e-mail you a notarized copy, and have the first check mailed to you."

"Thank you so much for your hard work. I really appreciate it."

"When I said I believed in you, I wasn't blowing smoke up your ass. I was dead serious, and Hollywood obviously believes in you too. We'll talk soon. Have a good night."

I finally made it. Through all the bullshit I went through, I gained Hollywood's attention.

I needed to be in my son's life permanently and my world would be perfect.

March

I sat in the courthouse outside the courtroom. Essence couldn't even look me in the eye. I was glad when the security guard finally called us inside.

Something felt off when I walked in the courtroom. The chubby security guard walked to the back of the room, and another man came out with the judge and sat next to him. I guess the other guy was there to record what Essence and I said.

The square-jawed judge's eyes were cold, and he looked at Essence and me before he shuffled the papers laid out in front of him.

"Why are we here today?" he asked and sounded annoyed. He lowered his glasses.

Essence raised her hand. The judge signaled for her to speak by waving his hand at her.

"Anthony is irresponsible and immature. I think we need to rework our visitation arrangement. I tried to work with him in the past, but we can't seem to agree on anything."

Her little act was award-winning.

The judge turned to me. "Well, do you have anything to say for yourself, son?"

"Yes, I do, sir." I cleared my throat. "I want to be a part of Tristan's life. I won't lie, Essence and I lack proper communication. She won't let me see him without a fight."

"I see here in the court documents that Ms. Dwyer had to call the police to her house because of you. Not to mention you've been arrested for a DUI." He stared at me and shook his head. The judgement flowed all through his voice.

"Yes, sir, I've made some mistakes in my life that I'm not proud of and—"

He cut me off. "The deeper I get into your file, the more embarrassed I am for you." His words jabbed at me like a knife.

I looked at Essence, and she was smiling. I had lost ground in the argument. It didn't look too good for me.

"Sir, I—" I tried to defend myself.

The judge cut me off again.

"You put your hands on the mother of your child, and you have an alcohol problem. You're the worst kind of person." He put his glasses back on. "I'll review the case notes before making a final decision."

He got out his seat and disappeared into the back.

"This is bullshit, Essence, and you know it. The only one you're hurting by doing this is Tristan," I said and slapped the table so hard that my hand stung.

"You should've played by my rules. Now you'll suffer the consequences." Essence walked toward me and stopped.

"What the hell is wrong with you? You're the one who up and left without fucking telling me."

She smiled. "I did leave, and I'm a crazy bitch too. Now I'm going to fuck you every way I can. There isn't shit you can do about it either." She blew a kiss at me.

I was going to call her a coldhearted bitch, but the judge came back out before I could say anything to her.

"After looking at different options and scenarios, I've made a final decision. Young Tristan needs a stable home environment where he is loved and taken care of." He stared at me, and then finished his statement. "I'm granting primary custody to Ms. Dwyer. The exception being one police-supervised visit per week for Mr. Porter."

Not believing what I just heard, I collapsed on the floor. I felt like my heart was ripped out of my chest and stomped on for good measure.

"Judge, please, don't do this." I got down on my hands and knees and begged him.

"I'm sorry, son. You've proven yourself to be abusive, irresponsible, and immature. I hope this teaches you a thing or two about responsibility," he said and walked toward the back. He spoke to us over his shoulder. "You two are free to go." The judge, the security guard, and the other guy left the room.

Even after everyone was gone, I sat there on the ground trying to come up with a plan to see Tristan more, no matter what the judge said. Then an idea hit me like a sucker punch.

I had to get me a lawyer.

March

I called my agent and asked him if he could put me in contact with a lawyer. He agreed and hooked me up with his lawyer who had a drinking buddy that practiced family law. Lucky for me, Anderson's lawyer's friend dabbled in entertainment contracts also at one time.

I met Marshall Covington at his office in Center City near city hall. I spotted the diamond-studded Rolex watch, three-piece suit, and his shoes looked like he bought them that morning. I hoped his abilities matched his appearance.

"You sure you can afford me?" Marshall asked with a whiff of arrogance.

"I wouldn't be here if I couldn't," I said and probably sounded snarky.

"Touché. Tell me what's going on and how I can help."

"I want more time with my son, but his mother is playing games. I need someone skilled in the courtroom with me so I came to you."

Marshall listened and nodded. "Give me a short version of the events leading up to this point and I can build a strategy from there."

"I can do that, but I also had a plan."

"I'm all ears."

"What if I could bribe her with money, but she didn't know I was bribing her?"

"You mean agreeing to pay her child support outside of a court agreement in hopes that with every subsequent increase, she would be susceptible to your demands?"

I smiled sinisterly.

"You creative sonofabitch," Marshall said, and we slapped hands.

"I'll draft up a place holder agreement, and we can edit the document if we have to."

"Sounds good to me."

"I'll contact you when I'm done, and I'll have a copy in your e-mail for approval."

I stood. "I appreciate the time."

"No problem. You'll get what you want in no time."

"How much do I owe you?"

"I'll e-mail you the bill as well," he said and smiled.

I walked out of Marshall's office to my truck smiling because I felt positive that he could help me straighten out my custody situation.

I drove to Essence's house for my first supervised visit and got choked up when I thought about seeing my boy.

With the baby bag over my shoulder, I hopped out of the truck. I went up her stairs and rang the doorbell.

When the door swung open, a tall, arrogant-looking police officer grilled me.

"Hello, Mr. Porter," the cop said and smirked. His breath smelled like shit, and I almost threw up because of the ungodly stench.

"Your visit ends at three-fifteen sharp and not a minute later, understand?" He tapped the face of his cheap watch. He was all business.

I wanted to punch him in the face and kick him in the balls. Instead, I smiled and nodded and walked into Essence's house.

On cue, she came downstairs holding Tristan. I couldn't believe how big he had gotten. Seeing him made me smile and calmed me down for the moment. I held tears back, although not by much.

She tried to hand him to me, but he cried and reached back for her. Seeing him hold on to her shirt and cry broke my heart.

"It's okay, boo boo. This is Daddy," Essence said and patted his back.

I took him from her and rocked him back and forth. It took me a minute, but I managed to hit him with some baby talk to calm him down. When I looked into his eyes, I saw myself in him. The feeling was priceless.

After a while, I pretended Tristan and I were alone. I fed him baby food and gave him his bottle. Holding him against my chest felt so right and natural. To me, nothing in the world was better than being a father. I rocked him to sleep and laid him in his crib. I kissed him on his cheek and forehead and inhaled his baby scent.

"I love you, son," I whispered to him.

I dug through his baby bag and pulled out a money order.

"This is for you." I handed Essence the envelope.

"Wow." Her eyes lit up like brake lights.

"Yup. And there's more where that came from." I gave her a fake smile.

"Good," she said, nodded, and put the money in her bra.

"I'll be back to see him next week."

"We'll see you then."

Having a cop there made me feel like a criminal. One supervised visit a week wasn't enough, and with Marshall's help, I planned to get what I wanted.

I refused to be a part-time father.

April

When I got the first payment for my screen-play, some of the pain I felt about my custody situation subsided. The money reminded me of what's good in life and where I wanted to go.

The check was for almost $34,000. I read the amount out loud and ran around my apartment screaming like a complete lunatic. I'm sure the people in my apartment building thought I was crazy as cat shit.

For the time being, I played along with Essence. I came to her house and spent my supervised hour with Tristan with a smile on my face like everything was okay. I made sure every time we met I increased the amount of money I gave her little by little. I noticed she became less of a bitch and more of a regular human being when the money increased.

When I got my next check for the screenplay, I could throw a lump sum at her to renegotiate our visitation terms. Our visitation paperwork stated that our agreement could be renegotiated as long as we both agreed to the new terms. I could play on her greed and hit the jackpot.

Once I deposited the money in my bank account, I set my future plans in motion. I enrolled into the first-time homebuyers program. Since I didn't have any serious marks on my credit report, they said I would be easy to work with.

While looking up foreclosures on the Internet, I looked at dozens of places before I found a three-story house in South Philly. The place had been in foreclosure for six months and was priced well below market value according to the information posted on the listing on their Web site.

The surrounding neighborhoods weren't in the best conditions, but I couldn't pass up the opportunity to be a homeowner, and especially at the price they were talking about. I signed all the paperwork they wanted me to, and then I had to play the waiting game.

Since I had been visiting Tristan, he learned to stand on his own. I loved being with him through his really important developmental stages. I would hold my arms out, and he would try his best to walk to me. Being a part of that made me a proud father. There wasn't a better feeling in the world.

As I drove to Essence's house, I smiled. I finally got up the nerve to ask my mother, Paul, and Mia to come with me on a visit. Why I didn't ask them to come with me before I have no idea. Paul and Mia were going to meet me and my mother there. She sat in the passenger seat as I drove.

"I don't condone violence, but I want to choke her," my mother said and shook her head.

I laughed and put the right turn signal on. "Trust me, Mom, I know the feeling. Every time I see her, I want to swing on her. As time passed, I've realized she isn't worth my time or my energy. Spending time with Tristan is the most important thing."

"How are you doing otherwise?" she asked.

"Well, I'm going to be a homeowner."

"What? Are you serious?"

"Yes, I am. I'm just waiting on the approval of my paperwork."

"I'm so proud of you, son. You're on your way."

"Thank you, Mom."

I parked across the street from Essence's house and gritted my teeth when I spotted the familiar police car sitting behind her truck. The cop car reminded me of how one-sided our arrangement really was and how eager I was to change things. She got to be around him 24/7, and I was stuck with one hour a week. I shook off the negative thinking; this wouldn't go on much longer.

As soon as my mother and I went inside the house, Essence came downstairs and handed Tristan to me. When he saw me, his face lit up. As I went to grab him, he reached his little arms out to me too. My heart swelled with happiness. I kissed him on his chubby cheeks and tickled his little stomach.

"Hey, buddy, this is your grandma." Introducing them to each other damn near made me cry. I handed him to her, and he went to her without hesitation.

Seeing my mother hold my son was a special moment. Like I always did, I imagined Tristan and I were alone. Only this time, my mother was there with us too.

My cell phone went off and pulled me out of the heartwarming moment. I stepped outside the house and took the call.

"What's up, Anderson?"

"They started shooting the movie. I thought you might want to know."

I smiled. "Thank you for letting me know, man."

"No prob. I'll keep you in the loop as they give me the information. You're on your way."

"Cool. We'll talk soon."

When I hung up with Anderson, Paul and Mia were parking their trucks behind my truck. Paul and I gave each other dap and a hug. I kissed Mia on the lips and hugged her tightly. Paul grabbed a huge stuffed teddy bear from the passenger seat of his truck.

My mother and Essence came outside, and Essence locked eyes with Mia. I noticed Essence's facial expression change, but she didn't say anything. I ignored her and introduced Tristan to Paul. I wouldn't let her mess this moment up.

"This is your uncle Paul."

"Here you go, little man," he said and handed Tristan the teddy bear. He hugged the teddy bear with all his might.

I passed him to Mia.

It was pure heaven having my family there with me as I spent time with Tristan. I had successfully reversed the situation. Now Essence was the one who couldn't do anything because of the cop being there.

A tinted out black BMW pulled up to Essence's house, and the driver beeped the horn twice. Essence gave Mia the evil eye as she took Tristan from her. Then she walked over to the BMW's passenger door. I looked at the New Jersey plates and shook my head. Now I knew who was in the car. Her little boyfriend, Austin.

Everyone took Essence's kiss to Austin as their cue to leave. I gave Paul dap and kissed Mia good-bye. My mother got into my truck.

I went over and kissed Tristan on his cheek. As I turned around to leave, the driver-side window came down.

"Long time no see, Anthony," Austin said and sarcastically smiled. I didn't knock his head off again because the cop was there with us. "Don't worry. I'll take care of shorty while you're gone."

I leaned into the window and said, "You lucky the cop's here, or I'd beat your ass again. It takes a real bitch like you to jump somebody."

"Just go, Anthony," Essence said, obviously siding with Austin, which didn't surprise me at all.

"Is there a problem here?" The cop walked over and asked us trying to sound authoritative.

"No, Officer, he was just leaving," Essence said, holding Tristan tight against her chest.

I looked at the cop and Essence, shook my head, and got into my truck without saying another word. The thought of Austin near my son pissed me off. I took a deep breath and remembered what I really wanted.

More time with Tristan.

"You okay, baby?" my mother asked.

"I will be, as soon as Essence gives me what I want," I said before I mashed the gas pedal into the floor.

It was time to finish off the plan.

April

With a lot of persuasion, Essence and I sat inside my lawyer's plush office in Center City.

"Hello, Essence, I'm Marshall Covington, Anthony's attorney. I appreciate you taking time out of your schedule to sit down and meet with us," he said and smiled politely.

"Nice to meet you too, sir, and it's no problem at all."

They shook hands.

He wasn't hip to her act, but I damn sure was. She sat there like she was sane, almost coming off as shy. I knew better. She might explode at any moment for any reason.

Marshall nodded toward me.

"I want to handle our problems outside the courtroom," I said to her.

"And why should I?" she asked with a raised eyebrow.

"The trade-off will benefit both of us."

"Okay. I'm listening." She folded her arms across her chest.

Marshall handed her a small packet of papers. I looked at Marshall, and he gave me a reassuring nod.

She looked over the paperwork and nodded.

"Everything looks good to me. When do I get my money?" she asked eagerly and rubbed her hands together.

I kept my facial expression neutral, but I was smiling on the inside.

Marshall pulled out a check for $5,000 from his breast pocket. Her eyes lit up like the Vegas Strip.

"As soon as you sign the agreement, the money's all yours," he told her.

Since Marshall was a notary too, he notarized the document for us.

Essence and I signed our names on the dotted lines of the agreement, and he gave her the check.

"I'm glad we got this done," I said flatly.

"Me too," Essence said and smiled without using her teeth.

When she finally left Marshall's office, I exhaled.

"What happens now?" I asked.

"I'm going to e-mail a copy to the judge and wait for him to send me the signed copy back. Once he does that, I will get you both a copy."

We shook hands, and all I could think about was spending more time with Tristan. Basically, our agreement stated that I would pay her $900 a month, I could see Tristan every other Sunday, Monday, and Tuesday, alternate holidays, and I had forty days with him in the summer.

I could make the money back, and I was willing to trade that for more time with my son.

Mission accomplished.

August

Four months later . . .

Compromised had a modest $45 million opening weekend against a $70-million budget. The movie had good reviews and good word of mouth so far.

I had never been big on social media, but the studio set up an account for the film. The opening weekend success made the movie a trending topic on Twitter.

Things were looking up for me. I had close to eighty grand in my bank account, and I got to see my son way more often. I was back on solid ground, and I couldn't be stopped.

Not only was the movie successful, but I closed on the house and paid $9,000 to seal the deal. Because of the renovations I had to wait a few months longer to move in. Becoming a homeowner made me feel like I was on top of the world.

I stood in front of my newly leased black-on-black Infiniti QX56 truck while on the phone with my agent.

"How do they feel about the numbers?" I asked eagerly.

"Since *Compromised* is outperforming expectations, I'm going to drive up the price of *Cold-Blooded*. They really want to buy it too. Thing is, we're going to need more than a hundred and fifty thousand. You deserve a raise, and if you get one, so do I."

"Now you're talking my language," I said and smiled.

"I'll set up a conference call with the executives and get the deal done."

"Cool. Let me know when you hear something."

As I got off the phone, Mia came out of the spinning glass doors at her job. She smiled when she saw me, and I hugged and kissed her.

"What are you up to?" she gave me the side eye after she got into the passenger side of the truck.

I shrugged. "You just have to trust me."

I parked the QX56 on a clean residential block despite the questionable surrounding neighborhoods. I blindfolded Mia before we got out of the truck.

Holding her hand, we walked up the steps of a three-story house; then I pulled the scarf off her eyes.

"Whose place is this?" she asked.

"This is ours," I said proudly.

"Don't play with me. Are you freakin' serious?" she asked, wide-eyed.

"Very much so." I put the house key in her palm. "I want us to move in together."

Her eyes watered. "What about our apartments?"

"I'll buy us out of our rental agreements. Everything will be fine." I kissed her on the lips.

"You got everything figured out, huh?"

"Not everything, but I'm getting there," I smiled.

She unlocked the front door and burst into the house. Once she got inside, she took off her shoes and disappeared upstairs.

I stood at the bottom of the steps, smiling. Now I had to cross my fingers that my agent could keep the gravy train rolling.

I was living my dreams like I always wanted to.

August

I had been calling my agent for two weeks, and he wouldn't pick up the phone. Pissed off, I parked in front of a drugstore with Tristan asleep in the backseat. My cell phone rang. The caller ID read Anderson.

"Wow. You're alive. That's good to know," I said sarcastically.

"You have every right to be mad at me. I didn't want to call and tell you the bad news about—"

"Bad news? What bad news?" I asked, cutting him off.

He took a deep breath.

My mouth went dry, and I kept tapping my foot.

"When I couldn't make a move with them, I had to call you. I tried my hardest, but the deal fell through. We couldn't come to terms on the money." He sounded defeated.

I breathed deeply. "Can you go back to the table and renegotiate with them?" My voice reeked of desperation.

"I can't. I tried. Things got pretty heated in the meeting. I have to wait until they cool down or go with someone else entirely. Besides, they aren't the only show in town." He tried to remain positive, but I became furious.

"I understand all that, but whatever you said reflects negatively on me too now. For your sake, you better find me another offer or find yourself another client," I said before I pressed the end button so hard my thumb hurt.

After I left the drugstore, I pulled up to my mother's house. With Tristan on my hip, I used the spare key and went in the house.

My mother came out of the kitchen as we walked in. She kissed me on the cheek and took Tristan from me. We sat on the couch.

"How have you been?" I asked her.

"Good. I can't complain. You?"

"I thought my agent had another deal on the table, and he told me today it fell through."

My mother smiled. "You've been the same since you were little. You want things when you want them. Waiting is a foreign concept to you."

"Yes, Mom. I'll admit I'm impatient. I can't help it."

"Well, you better learn some patience because you'll be disappointed if you don't."

I sighed. "I know. I'm going to try my best to calm down. I just want the deal to be over and done with." I rubbed my hands on my pants.

"That's not all that's on your mind, is it?"

I scratched my head. "No, it's not. I'm thinking about taking my relationship with Mia to the next level."

Her face lit up like the Philly skyline at night. "Are you sure? What brought you to this point?"

"A gut feeling . . . She's all I think about when I wake up in the morning and when I go to bed at night."

"Marriage is a lot more responsibility than just being a boyfriend. You do understand that, right?"

"I do, and I believe I'm ready for the added responsibility. Naturally, this is the next step for us."

"I think you will make a great husband, and she will make a great wife."

"Thank you, Mom."

"I'm only keeping it one hundred like you kids say."

"You're out of control."

"Have you picked out a ring yet?"

I smiled. "Not yet, but I plan to."

September

I walked into the his-and-her bathroom and relived myself. After I washed my hands, Mia wrapped her arms around me. Her hands on me always felt good.

"Good morning," I said and smiled.

"Hey, handsome." She kissed me on the lips and went to her sink.

Walking up on Mia, I towered over her. She stared at me lustily. We kissed and touched on each other.

With her back to me, I touched her smooth skin, kissing her collarbone and neck. I palmed her breasts, running all five fingertips over her hard nipples.

I pulled her panties down, and she helped me undress. She jumped up on the granite countertop and spread-eagle. She brought her clit to life and pinched her nipples. I rubbed myself against her until she begged me to go in.

I held on to her hips and went in raw. She was so warm, tight, and inviting. I went so hard our skin slapped together and echoed off the walls in the bathroom.

Still inside her, I carried her to the bedroom and held her against the wall and pounded her for ten more minutes.

Mia locked her hands and legs around me. I gave her a few more forceful pumps before we both ran out of energy. We looked at each other and shook our heads.

"What am I going to do with you?" Mia asked.

"You don't want me to answer that right now," I said and laughed.

My cell phone rang, and when I looked at the caller ID, it said, Anderson.

I scowled when I saw it was him calling me.

"What do you want?" I said with attitude.

"I've got good news," he said excitedly.

"I'm listening," I said flatly.

"Can you meet me at Morton's Steakhouse in Center City in like an hour?"

"This news better be worth my time. I'll be there in an hour." I ended the call without waiting for a response.

"Who was that?" Mia asked.

"My agent."

"What did he want?"

"He wants me to meet him at Morton's. He supposedly has some good news for me."

Mia stayed home with Tristan, and I went and met with Anderson at Morton's. When I got there, he was picking over a burger and fries. We shook hands, and I sat across from him.

"What's up?" He sipped his soda.

"I'm waiting on you to tell me the good news."

"Aren't we in a rush?"

"Pretty much."

"Okay. I'll get to it. I met with Thomas Lofton from Gold Standard Entertainment, and we have an offer on the table."

"How much are they talking?" I asked. I was still skeptical.

"Two hundred and fifty thousand. I wanted to push for three hundred, but I didn't want to screw anything up again."

Even though I was mad, I couldn't help but smile at the good news. He handed me the contract. "As soon as Marshall looks over everything, I'll get the contract back to you."

"No problem. Take as much time as you need."

"You should hear from me this week for sure."

"Sounds good."

I stood up and gave him dap and a hug. I wanted to do a cartwheel I was so happy. With more money on the way, I could definitely get Mia any type of engagement ring I wanted.

September

Having a healthy bank account, the woman of my dreams, a new car, and more time with Tristan gave me the peace of mind I always wanted.

Mia told me she had a surprise lined up for me, and I couldn't figure it out.

We drove in silence, and when we got to the Philadelphia International Airport I couldn't sit still. It wasn't until the woman on the PA system said, "Now boarding flight 127 to Las Vegas" that I almost lost it. You would've thought I was a little kid about to go to Disneyworld.

I didn't know anything about Vegas except what they showed on television, but I damn sure wanted to experience it.

After we got off the plane we hailed a cab to the Bellagio Hotel. The dancing water fountains in front of the hotel and the bright lights of the city had a magnetic pull of their own. You couldn't help but get swept up in it all. I had a pocket full of cash, a bad woman by my side, and seven days to show my ass in Sin City.

Once we got into our hotel suite, my jaw dropped to the floor. I turned around and looked at Mia in disbelief. She booked us the penthouse suite.

I had only stayed in a few hotels in my life, but nothing compared to this place. The room had a whirlpool, granite countertops, minibar, fifty-five-inch television, and electronic curtains.

She really outdid herself.

"You didn't have to do all this," I said as I put our suitcase in the master bedroom.

"Yes, I did. I want you to be relaxed. You deserve the time off. Shoot, we both deserve the time off," she said and smiled.

"You're absolutely right." I invaded her space and grabbed her ass.

"Don't start nothing, mister."

I kissed her neck and licked her ear.

"I made . . . I made us dinner reservations. We'll finish this when we come back," she said in between moans.

I softly bit her neck. "You damn right we will."

She managed to pull away from me. "You're too much."

Within minutes, we were seated in a dimly lit restaurant downstairs.

We both ordered the steak and Maine lobster. I wanted a drink like I wanted my next breath, but I restrained myself and had a glass of water with lemon instead.

I touched Mia's hand and looked into her eyes. Even in the dimly lit restaurant, she was the most beautiful woman I've ever known.

"If we never met, I don't know what the hell I would be doing right now," I said and shook my head.

"I feel the same way. I didn't know if I would ever meet someone worth my time. I dated a few guys, but none of them gave me the energy you do."

She spoke so passionately and honestly she turned me on.

"Well, you already know my history. I think it was meant for us to bump into each other that day at the coffee shop."

"Let's toast to finding each other."

We raised our glasses and touched them together. I finished off my water, and she drank her cranberry juice.

"I have another surprise for you," she said.

"Do you now?"

"Oh, I do. I'm going to visit the spa first so give me until 10:00 o'clock and meet me back upstairs," she said before she got up and kissed me on the cheek.

After I paid the dinner bill, I explored the Bellagio's entertainment.

I wasn't a fan of wasting money, but I spent a few dollars on slot machines and a couple of rounds of blackjack.

After I blew $150, I strolled into the Café Bellagio and bought an Espresso Macchiato.

I spent the rest of the time walking around the hotel, looking at the water fountains outside and exploring.

I came across Tiffany & Co. The store attendants gave me room to window-shop. There were many exquisite watches, bracelets, and rings in the display cases. One ring in particular caught my eye in the middle of the case. The small diamonds sparkled in the light, and I imagined the rocks on Mia's finger. I didn't have to wait. This was the one.

An avalanche of emotions hit me all at once. Although we were young, I wanted to grow old with Mia. There wasn't a better way to show my commitment to her than to put a ring on her finger and make us official.

Without hesitation, I dropped $7,500 on the engagement ring and walked out of the store smiling from ear to ear. I didn't plan on rushing the proposal, but I would always have the ring for whenever I was ready.

A little before 10:00 p.m., I went and took the elevator back up to our floor. The anticipation had my heart jackhammering in my chest because I didn't know what Mia had up her sleeve.

When I got into our hotel suite, I smelled lavender-scented candles and heard TLC's "Red Light Special" playing in the background.

When Mia stepped out of the bathroom dressed in a pink matching bra and panty set, I almost lost it. I wanted to throw her over my shoulder like a caveman.

"You like what you see?" she asked and spun around so I could see all of her.

I responded by grabbing her waist and kissing her passionately on the lips. She helped me undress. Minutes later, we were wrapped in the sheets making love under the moonlight overlooking the dancing water fountains outside. It felt like an out-of-body experience. By the time we were done, nine more songs had played and the candle had burned down quite a bit.

Mia slept peacefully as I held her in my arms.

I'm glad we came to Vegas.

October

I sat on the couch and looked through a pile of mail. Mia was at work, and I had the house all to myself.

The first envelope was a check. The next two envelopes were bills. The last one didn't have a return address printed on it.

That was weird.

I took a deep breath and opened the envelope.

When I saw *99.9 percent the father*, I broke down and cried because Austin was Tristan's biological father. I balled the paper up and threw it across the room. I sat there on the couch until there were no more tears to cry.

I felt an uncontrollable rage building within me.

Revenge was the only option. I wanted blood so badly I could taste it. I wiped my eyes and ran upstairs, got on my computer, and Googled gun laws and how to purchase a gun in Pennsylvania. Surprisingly enough, I found out the process wasn't as hard as I thought it would be. The gun store I found with Google Maps was close to my house.

I hit pay dirt.

I got to the gun store and rushed inside. The bell on the door jingled, and a silver-haired, overweight white man greeted me with a smile.

"What can I do for you, young man?" he asked like he was happy to have a customer.

"Hello, sir, I'm interested in purchasing a gun." My adrenaline spiked when I thought about killing Essence and her boyfriend in cold blood.

"Well, if it's guns you want, you've come to the right place, son. Let me show you some of our merchandise." He came from behind the counter and walked me over to a glass case in the back that held a bunch of different guns.

"Did you have a particular gun in mind?" the store owner asked.

"What do you suggest?"

"Depends on what you're going to use it for," he said uneasily.

I smiled. "Just for target practice. Nothing major, sir," I assured him.

"Then I'd suggest the .45-caliber pistol. At your size and your weight, you can handle the kickback. Plus the weapon is pretty popular."

"How much do I owe you?" I reached into my pocket.

He took the gun out of the case and wrapped it up for me.

"I can let the gun go for two hundred and fifty, and I'll throw in some free ammunition. How's that sound?"

"Sounds good to me." I gave him my debit card and waited for him to take payment and run my background check.

After a few minutes, my background check came back clean without any red flags. I signed all the paperwork and went on my way.

As soon as I got in my truck, I took the gun out of the bag. Holding the gun in my hand made me feel powerful. I put it in the glove box and drove to Essence's house in New Jersey.

I blew through all the lights and ignored the people who honked their horns and cursed at me.

I was a man on a mission.

I parked across the street from her house. I had a clear view of her front door. There were two cars parked behind each other in her driveway. I knew who the other car belonged to.

I put the clip into the gun like I saw on the Internet how-to video and put the gun in the small of my back. The faint sound of a New Jersey Transit bus rumbled behind me as I crossed the street. Essence's lights were on inside. She and Austin walked around in the living room.

When I walked up her steps, the porch light cut on, scaring the hell out of me. I banged on her door. My heart jackhammered inside of my chest. I touched the gun. I heard a song that sounded familiar. The song abruptly cut off.

I knocked again.

Austin opened the door and stood there smirking.

The anticipation of shooting them was killing me.

"What's up, Stepdad?" he smirked.

Seeing red, I clocked him in the head with the gun, and he crumpled to the ground.

I stepped inside the house and closed the door. Essence knelt beside Austin on the ground when she saw the blood on his head.

"What did you do?" she asked.

I pulled the slide back on the gun. "How long did you know his punk ass was Tristan's real father?"

"We only found out recently because we're getting married. He thought it might be a possibility, but I wasn't sure. Now that Tristan is his son, I'm glad." Suddenly, she cracked an evil smile.

"All I did was love you." My voice cracked with emotion.

"I wish I could say the same. You were just convenient at the time," she said coldly.

"Oh yeah?" I asked and shot Austin once in the chest and once in the head. The second shot made his head explode. I dry heaved when I saw his exposed bloody brain.

Essence had a crazed look in her eyes, and before I could react, she launched herself at me.

We landed on the couch. While we tussled, she punched me in the jaw and tried to grab the gun. I managed to elbow her in the head so hard she hit the ground.

Once she got herself together, she stood and said, "Go ahead and do it, you punk motherfuc—"

Looking her dead in the eye, I shot her twice in the chest. Blood sprayed on my face and shirt. She hit the ground with a thud. I dry heaved again when the coppery smell of her blood invaded my nostrils.

Then I wiped my face clean with my sleeve.

I wanted to start a family with Mia and for Tristan to be my biological son. The tears came when I realized that wasn't my reality, and it never would be.

I kept kicking her dead body. "You lying bitch!"

Breathing heavily, I ran upstairs to see my son one last time.

He slept so innocently. I wished I could take him with me. Memories of our time together flooded my mind.

I kissed him on his forehead and inhaled the scent of his baby lotion. I would remember that scent forever.

"I love you, son," I whispered to him.

After shutting the bedroom door behind me, I hurried outside and looked around cautiously. People looked at me funny because I was holding a gun and had blood on me.

Out of nowhere, police cars skidded to a stop near me.

When two officers spilled out of the car, I sprinted up the block. They yelled for me to stop, but the adrenaline wouldn't allow me to slow down.

Damn near out of breath and scared shitless, I cut through an alleyway and tried to shake them. My thighs burned as I struggled to breathe.

Three blocks later they were still on my ass. I saw a gate up ahead, and I was up and over it before they got there.

Seeing as though they weren't willing to jump over the gate, I kept moving without looking back.

A young guy was about to get into a Toyota Corolla, and I was all over him.

"Give up the car keys," I said calmly as I poked him in the ribs with the gun.

He handed over the keys without hesitation. Seeing the fear in his eyes gave me an overwhelming sense of power.

Once I got in his car, I mashed the gas pedal into the floor and blew through the yellow traffic light up ahead.

My phone went off with a text message alert. Without paying attention to the road, I looked at the screen.

The text message from Mia read, where are you? I have something important to tell you.

I dialed Mia's cell number, and headlights from an oncoming vehicle were the last thing I saw before everything went black.

Epilogue

The injuries I had from the car accident weren't life-threatening. I had a mild concussion and a broken arm. The physical wounds healed, but the emotional wounds never would. I wish I would've died in that accident; then I wouldn't have had to face a reality where Tristan wasn't my biological son.

I guess I should've been a combination of scared, remorseful, and depressed standing there in the courtroom beside my lawyer. I didn't feel any of those feelings. In the midst of everything crumbling around me, I tried to remain calm. I kept my facial expression emotionless. I was too numb to do anything else.

Once the judge said "twenty-five to life," the courtroom went bananas. The energy for me to plead my case disappeared a long time ago. The realization that I wasted years of my life I couldn't get back hit me hard, but I vowed not to show emotion. Not being there for Tristan, the

unborn child Mia was carrying, and my family
hurt me the most. I failed them because of my
piss-poor decisions. You didn't get a do over in
life, and I was living proof.

The judge banged his gavel because of all
the yelling in the courtroom. Paul had to be
restrained by the police when he tried to push
past them. Mia held my mother in her arms
because she had become hysterical with grief.

I whispered in my lawyer's ear; then I pulled
out the diamond engagement ring from Tiffany
& Co. and handed it to him.

"I'll take care off it," my lawyer said, smiled,
and patted me on the back.

Before I was handcuffed and led out of the
room, Mia and I made eye contact. I couldn't
stop the tears from falling. She cried too.

The last thing I heard Mia say was, "I'll wait
for you," before I was ushered out of the courtroom.

I knew she would probably find someone else,
but it didn't stop me from imagining the life I
would never get to live with her.